Books by Mary Catherine Campbell

Prince of Cwillan

Prince of Cwillan…"A very intriguing book
with unexpected twists"…Mary Ellen

"From the desert of Arizona to the old sod of
Ireland, 'Prince of Cwillan' is a journey into
fantasy adventure, romance, and tales of another world you will not want to end. Getting
to know the characters and their lives is like
meeting old friends for the first time. I can't
wait to continue the journey!…Judi F.

Tomorrow Is
A Long Time

Mary Catherine Campbell

Book Three
In the Prince of Cwillan Series
Lake of the Mirror

Eíst, amadan. Get up, or I will leave you here in the Fásach Mór, and let the Fear Dubh deal with you.

Déaglán, Lunasa, **Date Unknown**

PROLOGUE

Donal eased the steering board to the right; the boat made a slow turn. As the sail caught the breeze, Dobailein shifted the oars and relaxed. Wind powered, the curragh moved across Lough Faolán.

Brushing strands of his long reddish-brown hair off his face, Donal asked, "When did you start building this type of boat?"

"Our lord, Feargus, is having the monastery at Alibie restored. They found drawings for the boats in a dry hole in the wall. Who knows how many summers ago they were placed there," Dobailein said. "Did you sleep in the king's apartment?"

"No. Only one king ever slept there." Donal remembered the day he sat on the edge of the pool in the king's apartment, watching the goldfish swim in and out among the plant roots. "Did you see the goldfish?"

"Yes. Our good abbot said that Darlisca's army pried out some of the stones to release the water. All it did was lower the water level. Many of the fish lived. Where do these fish come from?" Dobailein asked.

"From Solaria. A tiny kingdom to the south, west of Moll-Dur."

Donal's thoughts turned from the colorful fish to the day he ran up the road to the Fortress of Cwillan. Niall had turned and yelled at Donal to try to catch him.

"Did they make you run up the road to the fortress?" Donal asked.

"All those that want to enter in as an Apprentice must run up the road." For a moment Dobailein frowned, lost in his own thoughts. It was gone in a heartbeat, and he said, "My father said that you were fast. I do not understand why you were required to do it?"

Dobailein didn't elaborate on how his run had gone or whether he'd made it as an Apprentice or not. So Donal said, "I was not required, but I like to run. Lord Niall challenged me to catch him. How did Feargus do? Did your father tell you?"

"He was as good as you," Dobailein said. "My brother, Lonán, thinks I might be too old to go with you. I will be eighteen summers on my next naming day. How old were you when you left Cwillan?"

"In my seventeenth summer." It was the closest Donal could get to his true age. He adjusted his long legs into a more comfortable position. So much had happened since that day.

Dobailein turned from watching a family of swans in the reeds close to shore. He was doing the math, and looked surprised at the answer he came up with.

"I mean no disrespect, lord, but that means you were very young at Boweayn."

"Yes, I was very young," Donal said. "Call me Donal. I am not your lord. Feargus is."

"I can read and write my name," Dobailein said, with pride.

"That is a good start," Donal said. As soon as Dobailein joined his household at Forest Lake, he planned to Anglicize his name to Devlin. "You will be tutored in my land as well. I want you to learn to read and write the name of each fortress and the lord who lives there, and his lady, by the time I return."

"I can do it," Dobailein said with conviction.

Something in his eyes told Donal a different story. Perhaps the young man wasn't sure he wanted to go on this adventure.

"If you are sure, I will give you the chance. Our cuaird will soon be over. Moya and I will be saying our farewells and leaving soon after our wedding."

Moya and he would be married that evening at Faolán. It was springtime, a good time to be married. They would be married again in Prescott, when they returned to Forest Lake, his other home.

"I will speak with your father. I plan to return before Samhain. Be ready to come with me then."

Dobailein gave him a slow nod. *He is doing this to fulfill Ciarán's wish, an old pledge, not his own,* Donal thought.

It was an old honor pledge made when they were young men. The war was over. On a day not unlike this day, they each pledged on their honor, and his father's sword that they would send one of their sons to be fostered by Cullan, Donal's name at the time. In return, he would send one of his sons to Cwillan.

Lord Rónán of Faolán had been the first to send his son, Martin, to be Donal's foster son. When Donal returned to Forest Lake, he would take Fionnbar, Lord Niall's youngest son, with him. Now Ciarán wanted his son, Dobailein, to go too.

There was more to this request, but until his former Guardian, or Dobailein decided to tell him, he would need patience.

Donal had not sent a son to his friends as pledged. Rather, he had left him behind. While not a deliberate move, it wouldn't surprise him if Feargus thought of himself as abandoned. Lord Niall had raised the boy prince to become king of the children of Déaglán.

What would Donal have done if he had known about his son? Would he have stayed? Probably. He put thoughts of what could have been out of his head.

On the far side of the lough, Donal turned the steering board again, bringing the boat about. Dobailein lowered the sail and put the oars back into the water. His muscles strained against his linen tunic as he rowed them back.

Ciarán waited for them at the bight where they would land. Near the shore, Donal slipped into the water and helped his former Guardian pull the boat onto the shore. Dobailein handed Donal his boots, unhooked the oars, and pulling out the mast, he stepped from the boat. When the boat was turned over, he placed the oars and mast beside it.

Feargus, Ard Ri of Cwillan, and Rónán, Lord of Faolán, seat of the clann of Guardians, came down to meet them.

Feargus stepped forward. "I am honored to be a guest at your wedding." Father and son embraced. When Feargus stepped back, he said, "We have not caught Mangan, but soon he will make a mistake, and we will catch him."

"Come," Lord Rónán said. "I have a meal prepared. We can talk over our ale."

CHAPTER ONE

It was a beautiful October day in eastern Cwillan. Donal walked along the beach at Lough Airgead, following the tracks of horses in the loose sand. Several of the horses had riders. He knelt down to get a better look. They had passed through here ten to fourteen days ago, long before he and his companions arrived. He continued down the beach until he was close to the inlet where the water from the upper and lower Silver Falls flowed into the lake.

On this side of the inlet, calf deep in the silvery-green water, his son, Rónán, fished with Vél and his youngest son, Beon.

Rónán had inherited his height and coloring. Donal's twins, Robert and Donald, looked more like the Long side of the family; heavy set with dark brown hair and eyes. His oldest son, Feargus, had light eyes and almost black hair like his mother, Aoife.

Vél stuck his pole into the sand and hurried to join Donal. They waded through the shallow water and stopped on the other side of the inlet.

Donal knelt down to examine the sand.

"What have you found?" Vél asked.

"Something was dragged up higher on the sand, where it is softer and dryer."

Vél climbed higher on the dune and examined the sand. "It looks like they buried something here."

"Yes," Donal said, standing. "Perhaps one of their horses broke a leg."

"This land belongs to the Ard Ri, but all are welcome to come here to fish or hunt. Do you think Feargus lost one of his horses?"

"Perhaps," Donal said. Though he didn't know why Feargus would come up here so late in the year.

Vél returned to his fishing. Donal was content to watch them. When they were done, he would clean and fry their catch.

The day was warm for so late in the season. The year would be over soon. Not for the first time he chided himself for not allowing enough time to take Rón to the Fortress of Cwillan so he could meet his older brother. He told himself they needed to get back as soon as possible. His son needed to get back to his tiny daughter, and Donal to Moya.

Lord Niall had been Donal's mentor, and later Feargus's mentor. He had taught them both well. What he had not been able to teach them is how to deal with each other.

Donal was never sure of his standing with Feargus. How would the High King react to meeting his younger brother?

He found a place to sit higher on the dune and sat down with his back to the sun-warmed sand.

From around his neck he pulled the pouch that once held his talisman. His horse head game piece and stones were in the rectangular glass case in his office, along with several relics he had found in the desert. From the pouch he pulled a smaller velvet bag. Inside was a teardrop-shaped silver pendant. The rounded end was bigger than a half-dollar coin, and thicker. On one side was engraved a running horse, the design on his standard. On the reverse side was Feargus's standard, an oak leaf copied from one taken from the Judgment Tree.

The pendant was his wedding gift from the Clann of Guardians. It must have taken them years to have the coin to commission the High King's artisan to execute it for them. He needed to find a sturdy silver chain so he could wear it. In the meantime, he would keep it in the pouch that once held his childhood treasures.

Donal placed it back into the pouch, hung it around his neck again, and dropped the pouch beneath his tunic. He leaned back, closing his eyes. He hated leaving Moya, but he had told Ciarán that he would come for Dobailein a week before Samhain. They agreed to meet at the western crossroads.

He smiled to himself, letting his mind run through his lovemaking with Moya four mornings back. Their June wedding came to mind. Rónán was best man, with Mary Rose Scanlon as maid of honor. Martin and Moya were kin, so he walked her down the aisle in the small chapel on St. John's Street.

His memories switched to them stepping from the chapel, husband and wife. It was almost the last time everything went right.

Donal's eyes snapped open. For a second he stared at the clouds drifting over the mountains on the far side of the lake. He shook his head.

Each problem led to why his son had accompanied him here to Cwillan. Donal sighed. There was no use fighting it. He closed his eyes again, seeing that horrible dream that seemed to have set everything in motion, he let his memories play out.

CHAPTER TWO

Donal stood at the front of the church in a powder-blue morning suit, his son, Rónán, also in blue by his side. The doors at the back opened, and the organist started playing as Liam O'Brien's granddaughter started down the aisle holding a basket of rose petals. As she walked, she scattered petals around her. Fionnbar came next with a pillow holding the ring. Mary Rose Scanlon stepped forward, a vision in pale blue, to follow them to the front.

The organist started the wedding march as Moya, escorted by Martin, stepped into the chapel.

Moya looked like an angel in white satin and Irish lace. Her floor-length gown, made up of three tiers, showed off her slim figure. Her auburn hair was pinned up, with a diamond tiara comb holding her waist-length veil in place.

She was nervous. Her hands holding the bouquet of white roses shook. Martin had his hand beneath the veil, along her back, giving her support and comfort. Those attending would think she was nervous about her marriage. In truth, she found her new life frightening.

Donal remembered the first time he saw an airplane, and later an automobile. He remembered going with Fred to a grocery store, how the rows and rows of food had stunned him. He had never seen that much food in one place.

After the ceremony, as they walked down the aisle as Mr. and Mrs. Tolan, Donal said a prayer to the Father. *Please Father, this time keep my love with me.* He touched his forehead, then his chest.

Donal was pleased to see his son Donald sitting with Robert Long and John and Robin Stills. He smiled at his son. Donald smiled back at him, gave him a thumbs-up sign. Perhaps Robert would come too. The chances of that happening were slim to none.

He was surprised to see Barbara Strickland sitting in the corner with her daughter, Jennifer. Barbara gave him a sad smile.

Outside, the street was crowded with families from Prescott and Middleton, here to wish the new couple well. Cake and punch would be served in Riverside Park along the Prescott River. Later, a reception would be held at O'Flaherty's, invitation only.

Donal had envisioned a quiet wedding held in the living room at Forest Lake, with a small reception there later in the day, but his partners, Mánus and Liam had spared no expense. They had arranged for a gown for Moya, the church, the cake, morning brunch, an evening reception, and to top everything off, a carriage and four matching white horses to drive them to the park.

When Donal protested the extravagance, Mánus reminded him that he was royalty, even if the town folk didn't realize it.

"Moya is your queen," Mánus said. "This should be a day to remember."

Their wedding day turned out to be picture-perfect, plenty of sunlight with a few fluffy white clouds in the sky, and low humidity.

Donal helped Moya into the open carriage that would take them over to Riverside Park. The rest of the wedding party, except for Mánus, Liam, Mary Rose, Fionnbar, and the flower girl, would follow on horseback. Donald would ride with his grandfather, Robert Long.

No, Donal thought, his problems had started at the park. Moya and he were walking back to the carriage when a young couple came over to speak to Martin. Donal recognized the young man, but waited for an introduction.

Martin introduced him as Keith Charles Little. The young man went by the nickname KC. He had had a front-row seat to the fight between his son Robert and Jason Strickland back in high school. Keith introduced the young lady with him as his fiancée, Tracy Lee.

"Congratulations, Mr. Tolan," Tracy said.

"Thank you," Donal said as he took the hand offered, flashed her his twenty-four-karat smile, leaned over, and kissed her on the cheek. "I'd like to introduce my bride, Moya."

Moya held out her hand and smiled at the couple.

"I thought you would be wearing a kilt, Mr. Tolan," Keith said. It was more of a statement than a question.

"It is a myth that the Irish wore kilts. In truth, Mr. Little, generations back we sent fabric over to Alba as a gift. My ancestors had no idea at the time that the Scots would wrap it around their waists."

Keith and Tracy laughed and moved on.

After Donal helped Moya up into the carriage, he looked around for Fionnbar.

"Has anyone seen Fionn?"

Martin and Cathal, who would ride behind the carriage, both said they hadn't seen him for a while.

"I'll go find him and meet you at Stan's for the brunch," Martin said.

Their cars had been left in the back parking lot of Stan's Roadhouse. There the trailers waited for the horses that would go back to Forest Lake. The carriage and four white horses would be returned to a stable near Chicago.

Clancy, the owner of Stan's Roadhouse, had a long canopy set up at the far end of the parking lot, under the trees. Beneath it, a long table was set up with food, fruit, and small cakes. Bottles of champagne chilled in buckets of ice.

Using his sword like a saber, Donal opened the first bottle, let the champagne gush out for a second. He tipped it up and filled glasses first for Moya and Clancy, then for Mánus, Liam, Rónán and himself. Jamie Ryan took Donal's sword and carefully cleaned the blade with a cloth before he slipped it into the scabbard and handed it to Seán Scanlon for safekeeping. Jamie opened the rest of the bottles the conventional way.

Martin rode up with Fionnbar riding behind him. They were just in time to enjoy a plate of Donegal boxty and a glass of champagne and to give a toast to the newlyweds, and Clancy, their host.

CHAPTER THREE

A t Forest Lake, Fionn was just coming into the main
hallway from the kitchen when Martin came in the
front door with a bundle of messages he called mail.
The strange device he kept in his pocket started to
make music. Martin pulled it out, slid it open, pressed a
button, and spoke into it.

Martin closed it and returned it to his pocket. "I
have to go below. Will you do me a favor?"

Fionnbar nodded, eager to help.

"Take this bundle of mail and place it on Donal's
desk. Don't disturb anything."

Fionn took the bundle and headed down the hallway. At the door to Donal's office, he knocked first and
waited, as he had been told to do, before he opened the
door.

The room was empty.

Fionn placed the bundle on the desk.

He glanced over at the wooden structure called a
bar and smiled to himself. Donal kept the most wonderful nuts in a container at the back. He did not think

his foster father would mind if he took just a few of the nuts.

As he was reaching into the container, the side door opened. Startled, he tried to hurry on the lid and spilled some of the nuts on the carpet. He ducked down behind the bar to pick them up.

Fionn knew he was really hiding. He backed up against the wooden bar and waited, his heart pounding in his chest.

When no one came over to where he was hiding, he leaned out. Alvin O'Brien was reflected in the glass sides of the sword case, in a pattern of overlaid images. He stood in front of Donal's desk, then turned toward the sword case.

Fionn was sure he was well hidden, so he didn't move back.

Voices out in the hall seemed to startle Alvin out of his thoughts; he turned and hurried out the same door he had come in. Donal and Martin came through the hallway door. Martin walked over to the bar. Fionn backed up against the wood again. There was a thud as something heavy was placed above him.

"I want a firm hand on Alvin," Donal said. "Let Carl know too. He is to be kept busy. I wasn't amused by his stunt of getting drunk at the wedding reception. Nor his off-color jokes the next morning."

"I'll see that he doesn't have any time to get into trouble," Martin said.

Martin's voice came from across the room, so Fionn leaned out to watch the reflections in the sword case.

"Do you think he will make it as an Apprentice?"

Donal sat down behind his desk and paused, staring at the sword case, before he said, "No. He is here because his father and grandfather want him to become an Apprentice. He would rather be partying in Chicago. If he makes any trouble, I'll send him back to Askeaton and let Mánus handle the problem."

"I'll go set up a schedule for him, and remind Carl that Alvin can't go off on his own."

The hall door closed. The only sound in the room was the rhythmic ticking of the grandfather clock in the corner.

"You can come out now, Fionnbar."

Fionn stood, placed the tin of nuts back on the bar next to a bottle, and came around to the front. He still had the nuts clutched in his right hand.

"What do you have in your hand, Fionn?"

"I dropped them."

Donal stood and held out a wastebasket toward him.

As he threw away the precious nuts, Fionn gave Donal a sheepish grin. "How did you know I was there?"

"Turn around and look at the reflections in the sword case."

Fionn's blood ran cold. Alvin had seen his reflection, as he had seen his. Fionn shuddered to think of what the young man would do to him.

"Are you all right, Fionn?"

Fionn turned back to Donal. "I am sorry for stealing the nuts."

"Is there a problem, something I can help you with?"

"No, not at all, Donal."

"I'll let Sally Brown know you would like a container of nuts you can keep in your room. Moya was looking for you earlier. Run up and keep her company for a while."

"I will, and thank you," Fionn said, backing toward the door. Out in the hall, he knew he was in big trouble. Alvin had seen him. Fionn hurried up the stairs to Donal's third-floor apartment.

ᏇᎀᏅ

After Fionn left, Donal turned on the sound system and began to sort the mail. In the center of the pile of statements and brochures, he found a handwritten letter addressed to Forest Lake. He opened it and found cut-out letters pasted together to form hateful words.

He could call Mánus Scanlon, but he needed to think this through first. It had been a long time since he last received a letter like this.

Why now, after so long?

When Martin came in to remind Donal about dinner, he was sitting at his desk with several sorted piles of mail and one envelope in the center.

"Problem?" Martin asked.

Donal looked up. "I received another one of those letters."

He opened his desk drawer, took out the letter, and handed it to his foster son.

"Damn, not this again."

I've been thinking about it, Martin. There is a key here to who is doing it, if I can only figure it out."

Donal pulled a slim folder from his file drawer and handed it to Martin. "This is what the profiler that Callie used to work with had to say about the other letters."

Martin glanced at the pages and handed the folder back to Donal. "He thinks that this person is between twenty-five and forty-five, educated, and that at some point he will act on his threats?"

"Yes, when they stopped, I forgot about it. But now I wonder, will he act on his threats this time?"

༚

Alvin took up a position next to the third floor grandfather clock. It had been bad luck that Fionn was in the office, but he wasn't going to let Donal's foster son spoil his grand plan.

As Alvin waited for Fionn to come out, he thought about why he was even here at Forest Lake. His father, Cathal, suggested to him that he join the Apprentice program before deciding what to do with his life.

What his father really meant was that it was time for Alvin to do something other than hang around the house all week and party with his friends on weekends. Alvin didn't want to join the program. But when he thought about it, by coming here it would get him closer to Donal Tolan. He wanted to get even with Donal and Martin.

And he wanted to do more than just send letters to the man he hated.

At one time Alvin was his grandfather, Liam's favorite. He was the fair-haired boy. It had all changed after the incident with the silver napkin rings.

Alvin loved shiny things, and the silver napkins rings were so irresistible and all he had to do is slip them into his pocket.

When his grandfather called him out about the napkin rings, he knew who had ratted on him.

Donal Tolan.

Donal had been there that day at the restaurant. He must have seen Alvin slip the rings into his pocket and told Liam.

Alvin had tried to bluff his way out of the problem. But the initials TG in fancy lettering engraved on the rings incriminated him. And so had the box of other shiny things he had borrowed over the years. He thought his grandfather was going to have a stroke when he found his grandmother's silver wedding ring in a velvet pouch at the bottom.

His mother, Peggy Joyce, had thought the ring lost forever when it disappeared a few years ago. Alvin still remembered the look of disappointment on her face at the discovery. The look Donal Tolan had put there.

Liam had humiliated Alvin by taking him back to the Tuscan Grille and had made him give the napkin rings back to the manager, with an apology.

His grandfather attitude toward Alvin had changed that day, he was no longer the favorite, and Alvin was sent to a doctor twice a week for counseling about why he liked to take things.

Now he had to do chores just like his siblings and cousins. Only Michael O understood him and they had become good friends.

Then there was the way Martin had manhandled him down in the stable the day after Donal's wedding. Hung over, Alvin had gone down to the second stable. He was sick there. Carl told him to clean up his mess. When he hadn't, Carl had called Martin down.

He remembered Martin's words.

"Clean up your mess."

"Carl can clean it up," Alvin said. "What are servants for anyway?"

"Carl isn't your gilly to take care of things for you. Clean it up."

Alvin refused again.

It was at that point that Martin lifted him off his feet and shoved him against the wall. "I am sure Mánus wouldn't mind coming down here."

Even though Alvin believed himself better than Donal and Martin, Mánus Scanlon was another matter. No one wanted to face Mánus.

"I'll take care of it," Alvin said.

When Fionn emerged from Donal's apartment, Alvin grabbed the boy before he had a chance to react. He dragged him through a door across the hall and shoved him against the wall.

The overhead lights came on. They were in a chapel. Alvin forced Fionn to sit in the last pew.

"If you tell Donal or Martin that you saw me in the office, you will be very sorry. Do you understand?"

Fionn looked too scared to answer. He nodded his head.

"I said, do you understand?"

"Yes," Fionn answered.

"That's better." Alvin let him go. "Now get out of here."

Like a scared rabbit, Fionn ran out.

Alvin checked to make sure the hall was empty before he hurried down the stairs. On the second floor, he went into the west wing and took the back stairs to the main floor. After checking the main hall, he went out the front door. Satisfied that no one would know he had been in the house.

Chapter Four

O ver the next week, Donal was aware of how quiet Fionn had become at mealtime. Alvin, on the other hand, was his usual smart-mouthed self. Could there be something between Fionn and Alvin? When Alvin became an official candidate to become an Apprentice and no longer had meals with them, Fionn had settled down, seemed his old self again.

Fionn had come back with Donal when he returned to Forest Lake in the spring. His foster son needed to see a doctor, and Donal made the earliest appointment available.

In early June, Donal took Fionn to see two specialists at Northwestern Memorial Hospital in Chicago. One doctor specialized in respiratory problems, the other in growth and bone development.

Martin drove them up to the Marriott in downtown Chicago; they would stay there for three nights. After seeing the doctors and setting up a schedule for tests, they had a late lunch in one of the private, upstairs rooms at O'Flaherty's.

"Well, it was good and not-so-good news today, Fionn."

"Donal, I have trouble following all those big words."

"Well the good part is they can help you with your cough, but you won't get much taller."

"Once, when I thought I would be an Apprentice, I worried about not being tall. Now it does not bother me so much."

"That's good," Donal said and smiled at his youngest foster son. Fionn had the Power; it helped him learn English at a faster rate than Moya. Soon Donal would have to start his training.

Donal went to serve more tea, and was surprised to find the pot empty. He took out his estate-linc and called downstairs for another pot of tea and some scones.

Fifteen minutes later, John Taylor, the barman, brought up the tea and scones.

"John, you should have had one of the cailíní bring up the tea," Donal said as Martin stood to take the tray.

"I thought it would be a good time to give you this," John said, and handed Donal an oblong padded envelope. "A young man left it at the bar on Sunday. He said to make sure I gave it to you the next time you came in."

"Interesting," Donal said as he examined the front. It was sealed, but not addressed to him or to O'Flaherty's, nor did it have a return address. Strange. "Thank you, John."

"That is interesting," Martin said after John went back downstairs.

Donal placed the envelope in his inside jacket pocket. There was something hard inside. He hoped it had nothing to do with the letter he'd received in the mail.

He smiled at his youngest foster son. "Fionn, what is the problem between Alvin and you?"

"There is no problem," Fionn said as he stared down at his plate of fries and half-eaten hamburger. "I am sorry about the nuts." He picked up his hamburger, then returned it to the plate without taking a bite. "Please, Cullan Donal, do not send me back to my father. You have done so much for me, and I could not bear to go back in shame."

Surprised at Fionn's plea, Donal said, "Fionn, I have no intention of sending you back. The only way you will go back is if you want to. If there is a problem, you would tell me, right, and if he threatened you?"

"No problem...Perhaps we could go now?"

Donal smiled at his foster son. He would have Martin talk to him later.

"Finish your food while Martin and I have some tea. Then we will go back to the hotel."

It was well past eight o'clock the next morning when someone knocked on the door of Donal's hotel bedroom. He had already showered and dressed. He called for the person to come in.

Martin stood in the doorway.

"Is something wrong?"

"No, it's Fionn. He would like to talk to you."

"I'll be right out."

Out in the spacious living room, Donal found that Fionn was also dressed. Martin placed a cup of tea with milk in front of Fionn, and a cup of black tea on the coffee table in front of Donal. Martin took his cup over to the bar, out of the conversation.

Fionn fiddled with his tea before asking, "Is Alvin, Mánus's son?"

"No, he is Cathal's son. Alvin is an O'Brien. He is only in the Apprentice program, and thus he has no standing at Forest Lake," Donal said.

"An O'Brien," Fionn said, almost to himself.

"Many of the O'Briens are descendants of Brian Mór. Some, like your father and myself, are, descendants of both Déaglán and Brian Mór."

"My sister, Rea, says it is not right to tell on one another."

Fionn was upset. He was slipping between Irish and English.

"If someone did something wrong, against your father or mother, it is not wrong to set things right." Donal kept his voice soft and reassuring to try to relax Fionn. "Or against the father of your heart," he added.

"I was after the nuts."

"Yes."

"He does not like me. I...I..."

"Who doesn't like you, Fionn?"

"Alvin."

"Close your eyes, lean back, get comfortable, and think about this. Tell me what has you so upset."

Fionn did as Donal asked. He leaned back on the plush couch, closed his eyes, and seemed to relax.

"Without opening your eyes, tell me what you see in your mind."

Fionn didn't answer Donal.

"Relax. You love those nuts. Try to start at a different point. What were you doing before you became upset?"

"Martin asked me to take your messages, mail, into your office and place them on your desk...I thought you would not mind if I took a few nuts." Fionn stopped and sat up. The color drained from his face.

"Go on, Fionn," Donal said softly.

"Alvin came into the room. I saw him in the glass, standing at your desk."

"The glass on the sword case, Fionn?"

Fionn nodded.

"What was he doing?"

"His back was to me most of the time. I do not know what he was doing. He told me later that if I told on him, I would be very sorry."

Donal glanced over at Martin.

"You can take your tea into your room, Fionn. I want to speak to Martin before we go down to breakfast."

Donal preferred to have room service bring up breakfast. For this trip, though, it was more important that his foster son was happy. He had decided to treat Fionn to the brunch offered each morning. It would make him feel special to have an omelet made just for him.

"Well, that was interesting," Donal said. "I didn't realize that Fionn was afraid of Alvin."

"And why would Alvin go into your office?" Martin asked.

"That is the real question."

⌒〜◯

Two days later at Forest Lake, Donal stood in front of his desk. Martin sat on the floor back behind the bar. The perspective would be different, since both men were taller than Alvin and Fionn.

Martin leaned out and said, "Fionn told the truth. He couldn't see what Alvin was up to. All I see is the reflection of you standing at the desk. The angle is wrong to see what you are doing."

"Alvin is a petty thief."

Martin stood and moved over to stand by Donal.

"What makes you say that, Donal?"

"He took my old punt coins out of the ashtray," Donal said. He walked over to the oblong glass case that ran along the front windows, referred to as a glass coffin because of its shape. He checked each of his possessions, and relics he had found in the Great Desert. Nothing was missing. The sword case had an alarm that would go off if opened.

Donal moved back to his desk and sat down. He gave a lot of thought to what he was going to say, before he voiced his opinion. "When I heard that Alvin was in here, I jumped to the idea that the letters were from him."

"I have to admit I had the same thought," Martin said.

Donal opened the desk drawer and took out the envelope. "It has a cancellation from a post office in Michigan. I think we can rule out Alvin."

"Unless he is working with someone."

"You mean like someone in the clan?"

"Yes."

"I hope not." Donal didn't elaborate on who he thought would help Alvin. From his jacket pocket, he removed the padded envelope. "I wonder what this is?" He pulled the flap up and shook out a small flash drive. "Now this is a surprise."

He opened the top drawer of his desk. He took out a black plastic box, plugged it in and inserted the flash drive into the USB slot. On the small screen, a dialog box opened and showed the operation as the flash drive was checked for spy devices, Trojan horses, or hidden programs that could infect his computer. When the box beeped that the drive was clean, he ejected it.

Donal slipped the box back in the drawer.

He opened his laptop. When it booted up he inserted the small drive into the USB slot. When the file came up he downloaded it onto his desktop.

He clicked the file to open it.

The first page was a proposal to Fisk and Fisk for a new mall north of Middleton, on what was once the Tyler Jenkins farm. There were two letters among the six documents. The company making the proposal for the mall was called Sundance Enterprise. Donal studied all six pages, then stood to let Martin look through the proposal.

When he picked up the padded envelope, he noticed that written on the underside of the flap was the word "kilt" in small blue letters. He showed it to Martin, then took the envelope and the flash drive and dropped them into a heavy-duty shredder, closed the clear plastic top, and pressed the on button. The machine, with a low whine, ground everything into confetti in seconds.

"Someone wants to build a mall north of Middleton," Martin said. It was more of a statement than a question.

"Yes. Interesting, I could think of several people who would have the money and influence in this area to get it done."

"Bad news for the Main Street merchants."

"I'm surprised this hasn't happened sooner. Years ago, Cynthia drew up a sketch of improvements for Main Street on both sides of the river. Pat Senior was Mayor then. She took the project to the city council. They looked at it, then shelved it as too expensive."

"Do you think it is too late to do anything?" Martin asked.

"Probably," Donal said. "As the leader of the Main Street merchants, I plan to fight it all the way. I don't want our downtown area to die like it has in so many small farm towns. Everyone will go to the mall. Though I wouldn't miss the teenagers that cause trouble down by the river behind O'Flaherty's here in Prescott." Donal paused. "The flash drive has to be from KC Little. Give him a call. Set up a meeting with him anytime next week."

"Here or somewhere else?"

"Here, or even O'Flaherty's. But I think he will want to meet on neutral ground. This could blow up in his face if Fisk and Fisk found out about what he did."

"You have to wonder how he received the information."

Donal did a secure delete of the information on his computer. He had what many doctors referred to as super autobiographical memory. He didn't need to keep the information.

Martin picked up his estate-linc and changed it for an outside call. He did a search for a number for Keith C. Little in Prescott or Middleton. When the number came up, he pressed the call button.

CHAPTER FIVE

Donal was wrapping up some work when Donald knocked at his office door and entered. The youngest of his twins moved over to sit in one of the chairs in front of his desk.

"Let's get comfortable," Donal said as he stood and motioned for Donald to join him in the living room part of his office.

He walked over to the bar.

Donald followed him over to better examine each label. "What is Screech?"

"Rum, from Newfoundland. Powerful stuff, I don't recommend it. I keep it for a friend. What's your pleasure?"

"I'll stick with the Midleton."

Donal placed two old-fashioned glasses on the bar, took down the bottle, and poured several inches of golden whiskey into them.

"I see you have Michael Collins."

"I don't recommend it either. Best to stick to good whiskey," Donal said, handing his son one of the glasses.

Donald was visiting friends in Chicago and had decided to stop by Forest Lake. He was flying back to Boston in the morning.

Donal sat down on the couch across from his son.

He waited, he would let his son get around to what was on his mind.

After taking a sip of his drink, Donald placed the glass on the coffee table between them. "When there is an opening at the Chicago office, I would like to be considered for it. Or if you ever decide to open an office here in Prescott or Middleton, I would like to be considered for that position as well."

"You should discuss this with your grandfather, Donald."

"Yeah, sure. Do you know, Dad, that Robert takes a two-hour lunch each day?"

"Yes, your grandfather has mentioned it to me."

"I got to thinking, if anyone else tried that, grandfather would have fired them on the spot, but not his grandson. So the question is why?"

"And what did you come up with?"

"That you told grandfather to keep him on."

Donal didn't really want to talk about Robert, but it was too late now.

"I asked him to keep him on, not told him to."

"Really," Donald said.

Donal doubted his son believed him.

"Talk to your grandfather. I'll talk to John Stills. When there is an opening, one of them will get back with you. I'm not sure your grandfather would be interested in opening an office in small farm towns like Prescott and Middleton. But I'll run it by him."

"I don't live with Robert anymore," Donald said. He obviously wanted to come home, but didn't know how to say so without losing face.

Donal had heard that the twins didn't live together. But he wanted Donald to think it was news to him.

"I hope it wasn't because of a fight?"

"No, no. We just see the world different now."

○○

On the same evening Donal talked to Donald, he also received a call from Callie Weston.

She was so full of life, it was always a pleasure to talk to her. "What can I help you with, Callie?"

"I was wondering when you will be in Chicago. I want to introduce you to Roger."

Donal had heard about Roger Orsnick from Seán Scanlon, Callie's boss. "Callie, I won't be coming up to Chicago for several weeks, if at all. Why don't you and Roger come down here? You can stay with us over a weekend."

"I better tell you, Donal. Roger would like to get a job with the Mánus Seamus Scanlon Corporation. Please don't let on that I told you."

"MSS can always use competent help."

"Would it upset Moya? You know, having me in the house?"

Donald laughed, "No, I don't think she will be upset."

"You didn't tell her?"

"Not everything. She won't mind, especially since Roger is coming with you."

༄

Two weekends later, Donal was leaning back against the front of his desk, watching Callie and Roger standing at the sword case. He was undecided about Roger Orsnick. It went beyond that he was ex-FBI. Or maybe that was the problem. *Is Roger trying to get to Mick Lafferty through me?*

Roger turned to him. "You can wield that thing?"

"Yes, I can."

Callie smiled at Roger and said, "I saw Donal and Martin put on quite a demonstration at a Celtic festival in Kentucky two years ago. He can wield it very effectively. Don't get in a fight with him, Roger. He's an expert."

Roger looked over at Donal, and for a second, a frown pulled at the corners of his mouth. Callie didn't seem to notice how she had put her comment, but Roger didn't like it.

He is wondering if he could take me. For the briefest moment, Donal's eyes went wide. Roger and he were fighting, in a place Donal didn't recognize. The vision flashed in his mind, and then it was gone. He shook his head to clear it.

"Is something wrong?" Roger asked.

"No."

"Having a vision?" Callie asked. "Donal is fey."

Roger leaned over and kissed Callie playfully on the cheek. Donal was sure he whispered something to her. He waited to see where this was going.

"Do you mind if I join the ladies in the solarium, leave you men to your whiskey?" Callie asked.

"Go ahead, darling," Roger said.

Donal reached into his pocket and pulled out his estate-linc, keyed in Martin's number, and pushed the button.

Once they were alone, Roger said, "Are you fey?"

"Men are never fey or sensitive to things." He didn't add that, from time to time, he did see things. It was part of having the Power.

Martin joined them.

Roger glanced at him, then over at Donal. "You don't need your minder, your bodyguard, here while we talk."

"Martin isn't my minder. He is one of my closest friends. What's your pleasure?"

"Glenfiddich straight up," Roger said.

"Midleton," Donal said to Martin.

When they were seated facing each other in the comfortable living room side of his office, Martin served the drinks. Roger was studying the chess set on the coffee table to his left.

"Your game?" Roger asked.

"Yes, it is an ongoing game with my partner. Whenever he thinks of a move he hopes to beat me with, he gives me a call."

Are you black or white?"

"Black," Donal said.

Roger reached over and picked up the black knight and studied the marble game piece for a minute. "Nice set," he said, then replaced the knight on the wrong square.

Even if Roger had upset the whole chessboard, it wouldn't matter. Donal had the board memorized. He reached over and placed the knight where it belonged.

"How are things up in Chicago?" Donal asked.

"Fine." Roger paused, before he said, "I would like to join MSS."

It would be better if he didn't hire Roger. He didn't want the vision he saw to come true. All Donal said was, "You should put in an application with Seán Scanlon. He runs MSS."

Roger took a sip of his drink and put it down on the coffee table. "I thought I would avoid the middleman and go straight to the decision maker."

"You realize new employees come in at entry level."

"Why?"

"That is our policy."

"You know it is against the law to discriminate because of race, creed, or not being a Catholic." Roger looked him straight in the eye. Donal didn't flinch.

Donal kept what Martin always referred to as his "king face" on, giving no clue to what he was thinking. "We never ask about a person's religion when we hire at MSS, or for the restaurants."

Roger looked surprised. "Just so you know my pedigree, my maternal grandmother was Irish."

Donal decided to let the comment pass. *Roger is trying to let me know he is one of us. Well, he really isn't.* Besides, Donal didn't care if Roger's grandmother was Queen Maeve herself. He wouldn't be getting a job at MSS.

"Anyway, we are all adults here," Roger said. "Callie is young and beautiful. We both know how she got into the Irish version of the 'boy's club' at MSS."

Donal knew at that point he didn't like Roger.

"Are you always so blunt, Mr. Orsnick?" Martin asked as he came around to stand in front of the bar.

Roger turned so he could face Martin. "He can talk too? Interesting." Then he turned back to face Donal. "I have a lot of experience that MSS could use."

Before Donal could answer Roger, a knock came at the hall door.

"Come in," Donal called.

Fionn came in and announced that they were ready in the living room. Donal stood, putting off answering Roger. "You'll enjoy this. Johnnie is an expert fiddle player, a friend will do a few vocals, and my son, Rón, is going to accompany him for a few instrumentals on the piano."

~

Meeting Johnnie Coffey had been a strange affair. Donal was getting ready to head home in July when the county sheriff, Mark Sims, called him.

Mark and he were friends from back in the days when Donal came back to live in Prescott and Mark was deputy sheriff with his uncle, Max Sims.

"Mark, what can I help you with?" Donal said.

"We had a little trouble at the Riverside Park earlier."

Not sure what it would have to do with him, Donal said, "Anything I can help you with?"

"We picked up a panhandler camping in the park. He doesn't speak too much English, keeps talking in a foreign language. My deputy thought it might be Irish."

"Martin and I were just about to leave. We'll stop by the jail before heading home."

Mark waited for Donal to arrive. He took them to the cells in the back. In the first cell, a man sat hunched over, deep in thought.

"What's his name?" Donal asked.

On hearing Donal's voice, the man looked up. He was in his early thirties. He stood, pulled the cap from his head, and mumbled something in Shelta, the language of the Travellers.

"His name is Johnnie Coffey."

"Please, lord," Coffey repeated in Irish. "Don't be mistaking me by my Munster name. My great-grandfather came from Ulster, near Lifford, same as yours."

Surprised at his words, Donal said, "You're a musician, aren't you? I heard you in Boston last year."

"I played the fiddle with the Dublin Paperboys. We were playing at the Black Rose in Boston. Later we moved on to Toronto. We played at Dora Keogh's place. The next pub wasn't as good. The manager took a dislike to me. I left rather than let the band get the sack. You can't trust a Sasanach."

Martin handed Donal his estate-linc with the information on Johnnie Pádraic Coffey, from Limerick, Ireland. It didn't mention the trouble in Toronto.

"What is the name of the place you had trouble at?" Donal asked.

Johnnie gave him the name, and Donal fed the information into his estate-linc.

"Did you know that they have a new fiddle player? A young man with the same last name as the manager?"

"Nothing would surprise me."

"I'll pay his fine," Donal said, making his decision. He handed the estate-linc back to Martin.

"He hasn't any visible means of support, nowhere to live," Mark said.

"Martin, call St. Anthony's. Let's see if we can get him a bed there for the time being."

It turned out that Johnnie could speak English, but chose not to. He cleaned up nicely. Donal had him checked out at Prescott General before he asked Thomas to try him out as a fiddle player on Sunday night in the side room.

Two weeks later, a girl named Siobhán Dunn showed up to do a few vocals with him. Both Johnnie and Siobhán helped out by busing tables, asking for no extra pay.

ᘛᘚ

In the living room, Johnnie waited by the piano, his fiddle at the ready. Rónán sat on the piano bench.

Next to him sat Siobhán Dunn, her legal name turned out to be Sally Ann. Moya was sitting near the French doors to the solarium. Callie sat with Sally Brown and Mrs. Murphy on a couch to the right. Fionn went over and sat next to Moya.

Johnnie was so good that Donal was toying with the idea of setting up his own music company: Ireland and Beyond.

Traditional music, not as big a seller as the more commercial bands and singers, was in decline. Like his native language, Donal wanted to keep it alive. If he did, he would promote Johnnie, Siobhán, and other traditional artists.

The traditional music played by Johnnie, with accompaniment by Rónán and haunting vocals by Siobhán, seemed lost on Roger Orsnick, but everyone else seemed to enjoy the afternoon.

∞

"Good morning."

Donal glanced up from grooming Ghost Warrior. "Good morning to you too, Callie." He flashed his twenty-four-karat smile at her. As usual, she looked beautiful. She had cut her blonde hair to just below her shoulders. She was a vision with her stunning video-star good looks.

"I was looking for you earlier this morning. Carl said you might be in church."

"I was. It is the first time in years we had a service up in the chapel." He smiled at Callie again. "I didn't invite you or Roger, because it was in Irish."

"She is wonderful."

Donal stood up after checking Ghost Warrior's right fore hoof. "Moya?"

"Yes. She is a real lady. No hard feelings toward me, she knows she won."

Donal didn't know if he should smile or be offended. "You make me sound like I am some sort of prize-catch the brass ring, or find the prize in a box of Cracker Jack, and you win." He paused, then said, "I think this was a bad idea."

"Sorry, I didn't mean it that way. And I didn't come here to try to resurrect old times between us. I knew it was over years ago. Your life here is different, and I would never fit in, not like Moya will."

Donal checked the left fore hoof before he stood up again. "I meant bringing Roger here."

"I feel the same way, now that you mention it, Donal."

"I can't help feeling he is trying to get to Lafferty through me."

"Do you know Michael Lafferty?" Donal gave her a surprised look. "I'm sorry, I didn't mean it like that, either. It's just that Lafferty is on the other side."

"We are both lads from Donegal. I met him once at a restaurant in Navy Pier. I don't know him other than that brief conversation."

"Are you sure the feds aren't trying to get to you, Donal?"

"There is always that possibility. If Roger and the feds think we are a bunch of dumb Micks who got lucky, then they have a big surprise coming." Changing the subject, Donal said, "How are things at MSS?"

"Seán asked me last week if I was interested in being security for a courier. I wasn't sure if it was something I would want to do, since I would be out of the country for a few weeks."

"He did mention to me that they had an inquiry about the job. It isn't something MSS usually does."

"Roger and I will head back up to Chicago after lunch. Seán will want to know one way or the other tomorrow."

"I guess, Callie," he said, facing her, "it comes down to how serious you are about Roger." Mentally, he was thinking of who he could send out with Callie. Someone like Tyler Monaghan would be good, single and right around Callie's age. "If your relationship isn't serious, take the job. I hear New Zealand is beautiful."

"I was serious about Roger. Now I am not so sure. It seems like his real interest in me is to join MSS."

Donal knew it would be best for everyone if he didn't hire Roger. But he remembered an old saying, "Keep your friends close, and your enemies closer." Perhaps he should have Roger where he could keep an eye on him.

Before they could go on, Roger called Callie's name out in the stable yard. A minute later, he walked into the stable. "Well, well, here is where everyone is hiding."

"Just finishing up with my horse," Donal said as he led Ghost Warrior into his box stall and closed the lower half door.

Roger gave him a look that said he didn't believe it for a second.

"Excuse me," Donal said, "while I get a couple of carrots out of the fridge."

After Donal fed the carrots to Ghost Warrior, he stepped over to the sink by the office wall. He washed his hands and face. As he dried off, he glanced in the mirror. Roger had moved over to where he could see him. Their eyes locked again. Donal didn't flinch. *He is still wondering if he can take me,* Donal thought. When he was dry, he took his shirt off the hook to the left of Ghost's stall and put it on over his undershirt.

Rónán walked in, breaking the tension between them.

"Hi, Callie, you're a breath of sunshine on this fine day. Morning, Roger, Da." He kissed Callie lightly on the cheek and turned to Donal. "Sally has everything set up in the solarium."

"We better go up," Donal said. "Roger, I'll have Seán send you an application. But as I said yesterday, it will be at entry level."

CHAPTER SIX

Morning mist hung over Lough Airgead. The mist moved in lazy swirls as a light breeze from the south disturbed the smooth surface of the green water. Donal ran along the beach toward the Southern Pass. The air was cool. He wore only a medium-weight tunic over his leggings. His hair was tied back to keep it out of his eyes.

Donal was surprised that the mild weather had held this late in October. He reminded himself that any day now it would grow cold and snow would fly.

At the headland he slowed, walked for a few feet, then turned and started back to their camp. It was still early. He hoped to return before anyone else was up.

In his mind, he returned to his memories of why he had brought his son to Cwillan.

The memory of the horrible dream made his blood run cold in spite of the heat from running.

He let the dream play out in his mind.

The bright red standard was lifted into the afternoon sunlight. It looked as if it was stained with blood. Unseen hands planted it in the center of the battlefield. Around Donal came the cry of anguish from his men, while a cry of victory rose from their enemy.

Somehow, he and Feargus had been split up. *Of course, divide and conquer.* From his vantage point, he couldn't tell where Feargus was, or what had happened to Ciarán and Lonán.

Tinreach, Feargus's silver-white stallion, ran past, riderless.

The man to his left shouted, "All is lost."

"Not yet," Donal cried. He shouted to his men to rally them. They had to see how things stood with Feargus.

Funny, I don't know which enemy we are fighting.

With a strange perception, now alone, he ran across the battlefield. No one seemed to see him. All around him, men fought. Yet no one tried to stop him, no one challenged him.

He almost reached his son.

Almost.

Horrified, he watched as his son went down. The warrior standing over him pulled the blood-red standard from the ground, ready to plunge the point into his son's heart.

"Dear Father, help us."

Moya woke him when he sat up in bed and cried out to the Father.

"Grá, what is wrong?"

For a second, relief flooded his consciousness. It was just a bad dream, nothing to worry about. Or was it?

"Just a bad dream," he told Moya.

It was more than a bad dream. It had unnerved him. He wanted to get up and go downstairs and call Brid. What could a nightmare like this one mean? Was his son in trouble?

At first light, Donal called Brid.

He smiled when a young, sleepy voice answered the phone.

"Hello?"

"I'm sorry to wake you, Rhyianna. I thought your mother or father would be up by now."

"Donal," she said, her voice brightened. "Mother and Dad are up in Ludington on a mini vacation. I'll just run downstairs and get the number for you."

"Don't bother, Rhyianna. When you talk to your mother, let her know I called."

Listening to Rhyianna's voice over the miles brought back the sound of another voice that had come to him over the years.

"Have her give me a call."

Brid called him back an hour later.

"Donal, you needed to speak to me." It was statement, not a question.

"When will you be home? We need to get together."

"Come by next week. Is Tuesday good for you?" From the sound of her voice, she was looking at her calendar.

"I'll see you on Tuesday."

CHAPTER SEVEN

"Are you awake?" Rónán asked, having come up from the beach to join his father.

"Yes," Donal said, opening his eyes. "I was just thinking about home, Rón." Brid had tried to calm Donal. Yet her words neither calmed him, nor upset him further. He shook off the memory of his meeting with Brid. He needed to concentrate on the here and now.

"I thought this was home?" Rónán asked.

"I have two homes, here and Forest Lake."

Donal stood as Beon came running up the beach with a string of fish. Donal took the fish. "You did well. Go help your father get the fire ready."

Beon ran down the beach toward their camp.

"You okay?" Rónán asked Donal.

"Yes. Why do you ask?"

"You look as if something has happened to upset you."

"I am fine, son. Come on, I have fish to clean and fry."

They walked down to a flat rock at the water's edge, set here in his father's or grandfather's time to have a place to clean fish. Donal knelt and cleaned the fish with the efficient movements of a man who had done it many times.

"You need to teach me how to do that," Rónán said.

"Tomorrow, I'll show you how."

"Have you ever used a gun?" Rónán asked as they walked back to their camp.

"Yes. Callie taught me. I learned enough to know how to load and use one if I had to. Martin carries one anytime we are away from Forest Lake."

"I didn't know that."

"It was a hard decision for me to make, whether any of the Guardians would carry a concealed weapon."

"Speaking of Callie, she called while you were out, just before we came to Cwillan."

"Did she leave a message?"

"She said she would be out of the country for a few weeks. She had a job to do for MSS. After that, she planned to take her vacation."

Good news, thought Donal.

When their meal of fresh fish was over, Rónán walked over to the top of the beach path, and a few feet down, to a place he could watch his father.

Vél came down to stand by him. "Donal seems to have much on his mind. He will find a quiet place to think things out."

"I worry just the same," Rónán said. In English he mumbled, "I'm the one who messed up, and he knows it. Why didn't I tell him?"

"Come," Vél said as he gave him a puzzled look. "Help me with the horses."

Rónán knew Vél had heard him but didn't question him about what he had said.

❧

Donal walked along the top of the sand dune and sat halfway down the beach as the day waned. The jagged mountain peaks on the far side of Lough Airgead caught the last rays of the setting sun, bathing them with golden light. At this time of year, there should be snow on the peaks, but the good weather had held even at higher elevations.

The lake was quiet. Not a ripple marred its surface. It looked like the common name given to Silver Lake: Lake of the Mirror.

His thoughts turned back to what had happened in Prescott.

Donal went through his memories and the thoughts he'd picked up from people like KC Little and Fionn, then continued with his meeting with KC Little.

CHAPTER EIGHT

Keith Charles Little studied his reflection in the mirror. He made another adjustment to his tie, brushed back a stray hair, practiced a few smiles, and sighed. He was stalling, and he knew it. He walked to the door and wiped his sweaty palms on a towel before he turned off the light in the old-fashioned bathroom.

For years his mother had tried to get him to update the old farmhouse. It was his now. He could do with it what he wanted to, keep it just as it was when he was a small boy, when his grandfather lived with them. Usually, thinking about those days always put him in a mellow mood. Not today, he was too nervous about the meeting.

He sighed again.

Downstairs he found his fiancée, Tracy, out in the screened-in porch, eating breakfast. She gave him the once-over and shook her head. "You look like your going for a job interview."

"I just want to look good."

"I had lunch at O'Flaherty's in Chicago, with a friend," she said. "Before we met. Donal never over-dresses, dark slacks and a white shirt, sport coat."

"Well, it never hurts to look good."

"You should have taken him up on the offer to go out to Forest Lake." Tracy poured him coffee, moved the sugar bowl and creamer closer to him.

"Why?"

"So you could tell me what the house is like."

"It's big," he said. "I know what you want."

"What?" she looked at him with her big blue eyes, guileless.

"I told you before, I never hung out with the Tolan twins, and Rónán was several grades below me. So I can't introduce you to him."

Tracy gave him another smile. She was rattling his cage, to take his mind off the meeting this morning. He smiled back at her. It had worked, in a way.

"I saw Rónán at Grant Park last summer. He's really good-looking, looks a lot like his father. There was a girl with him. She's a looker too. She seemed, at the time, to be very shy, or afraid."

"Anyone I might know?" Keith asked.

"Couldn't say, I only recognized him from the news. They had a party at O'Flaherty's. He was standing outside the front door, by the flags, with the new mayor, Mr. Daley."

Keith didn't tell her he was afraid to go to Forest Lake. What if the firm his friend Vince worked for found out about what he had done? Now the information was in Donal's hands.

Let him decide what to do with it.

He had been surprised when he received the call from Martin Rinn. They agreed on Stan's Roadhouse as a place to meet. Why had Vince shown me the file?

Why had he left the room, giving me a chance to download a copy of the information, in reality stealing it?

On the drive over to Stan's, he thought about Donal Tolan. They had never talked until that morning at Riverside Park. The only contact he'd had with the family after the fight Robert Tolan had with Jason Strickland was through their lawyer, Dominic Monaghan.

Donal was an enigma. On the surface he looked calm, even soft, but when you looked into his eyes, you knew he was hard as steel. There was more to Donal C. Tolan than what showed on the surface: pub owner, thoroughbred horse breeder.

Old Man Strickland was a fool, an amadan, as his grandfather would have called him, taking on someone like Donal.

Funny, Donal had never married again, until now.

What was Mrs. Tolan really like?

Keith turned his late-model Ford into Stan's lot, parked on the side, and entered the old building. It was gloomy inside after the bright sunlight of the beautiful summer morning.

One of Clancy's waitresses glanced up from her work. "We won't be open for another hour."

"I'm supposed to meet someone here."

"It's okay, Margo," Clancy said as he came down the stairs from the second floor, where he lived. "Do you want a private booth?"

"Out here is fine." Keith had never sat in one of the private booths from back in Prohibition days. They were in the back somewhere.

Clancy nodded, and led him to a table in the far corner, inquired if he could bring him something. Keith said coffee would be fine. He sat down with his back to the wall, something he had learned in high school-sit where you could watch the room. Margo brought him a mug of coffee, sugar packets, and cream.

Keith glanced at his watch. He was early.

At exactly ten, the side door opened and Donal stepped into the room followed by Martin. Tracy was right. Donal was dressed in dark slacks, white shirt, and a gray sport coat. Martin was dressed the same. Keith undid his tie, slipped it off, folded it up, and slid it into his pocket.

Donal went to the bar first, to talk to Clancy, before he came over to the table. Margo came over again to take Donal's and Martin's orders. After she brought over tea for both men, she went into the back.

The silence that followed made Keith uncomfortable.

"What you did is against the law," Donal said as he stirred his tea. "Now if they have some kind of security tracking system on their computer, you could be in deep trouble."

"More likely, my friend will be in trouble. He could rat on me, but I don't think he will. It's not as if I'm stealing government secrets."

"The real question is why you sent the information to me?" Donal asked.

"Because someone needs to do something about the mall."

"I can move my pub into the new mall. So can Sam Cheng and several other merchants. So I'll ask you again. Why? Why not take it to Strickland, or one of the other country club members, or even our lord mayor?"

Keith smiled at the title given to the mayor. "Why?" His good mood hadn't lasted long. He had to fight to keep his cool. "It wouldn't surprise me to learn that Strickland is behind the new mall. I moved to Chicago three years ago. I had a position with a security firm. I was on my way up. The only problem, I hated Chicago, hated all the noise, the traffic. When my mother died, I came home.

"Why do I care? Prescott is my hometown. My family moved here after the Civil War..." Keith stopped, not sure he was making sense. He stood to leave. Perhaps he had been wrong about Donal Tolan.

Donal asked him to sit down again.

"I was thinking of having you join my security company outside of Chicago. I guess that is out of the question."

Surprised, Keith stared at Donal. He had never heard of him running a security company.

"Perhaps you might consider working for me anyway. I could use someone local."

"I have a business set up already, Mr. Tolan."

"Please call me Donal. This would be in addition to your business."

Donal didn't humiliate him by reminding him that spouse surveillance in a small farm town wasn't much of a business.

"You could work for me on a retainer basis and still keep your office open in Prescott."

"I don't know." Keith wanted to say yes. With a steady income, he could fix up the exterior of the farmhouse, even plant the south acreage. What made him hesitate? "Will you stop the new mall?"

"Nothing is certain in life, Mr. Little. May I call you Keith?" Donal said.

"Yes, or call me KC. And in the meantime?"

"See what you can find out about Sundance Enterprise."

From his inside jacket pocket, Donal pulled a business-sized envelope with a business card attached. He handed it to Keith.

"This is a down payment, expense money to get you started. If you need more, let Martin know. His personal number is on the back of the card."

Keith stood, shook hands with Donal, then Martin. He thought later, *I must have been mistaken about the tingling sensation when I shook with Donal.* He dismissed the thought, put it down to the excitement of having a paying job.

He didn't open the envelope and look at the check until he was parked behind his office. He gave a low whistle. As soon as possible, he would call Tracy and bring her up to date. They wouldn't have to worry about the upkeep of his office or the farm for a long time.

Keith had only one client to talk to this afternoon. After that, he would see what he could find out about Sundance Enterprise.

CHAPTER NINE

Donal moved Moya's arm off his shoulder and eased over. He had almost made it out of bed when he heard her sleepy voice.

"Mo ghrá, it is early."

"I need to go into town today." He needed to stop by the China Star and talk to Sam Cheng and his daughter, Lily.

Moya ran her fingers along his arm, her smile inviting him to stay a little longer.

"What will everyone say when we are late for breakfast?" he asked.

"Martin and the Ladies know that we are newlywed and want to spend time together."

Moya referred to Sally Brown and Mrs. Murphy as "the Ladies." It was catching on.

Donal smiled at his bride of only weeks. He lifted the blue-and-green duvet with matching blue sheets and slipped back into bed.

෴

Donal and Martin didn't get to O'Flaherty's until after two o'clock in the afternoon. Donal was surprised that a man by the name of Walter Stevens was waiting to talk to him.

Tabitha handed Donal his business card.

He looked it over and said, "Walter Stevens? Sales Manager? I wonder what this is all about."

She told Donal that she had Mr. Stevens seated in a back booth.

"Let him know I am here and will join him in a few minutes." It looked like he would have to put off talking with Sam Cheng and his daughter till later. He asked Martin to give Sam a call, apologize for him, and set up a new time.

Walter Stevens looked like a prosperous young businessman, gray Brooks Brothers suit, white shirt, and conservative tie. After the introductions, Stevens got down to business.

"I brought a couple of brochures and a layout of the complex. Your son is wise to make an investment so early in the development of Fountain Park."

At first Donal thought he must be talking about one of the twins, until Stevens pronounced his son's name as "Ronand."

"Perhaps you might be interested in making an investment with us too, Mr. Tolan."

Stevens spread out a stylized map of the complex. There were a dozen condominiums clustered around a circular commons with a tall fountain at the center. Only one building was near completion.

"Exactly where is Fountain Park located?" Donal asked. He had an idea that the condos were connected with the new mall.

"On the Middleton side of the river, well north of town. Country living at its finest," Stevens said, and handed Donal a brochure depicting the elevations and interiors of each model.

"Very impressive. So how do I figure in on this? At the moment, I'm not looking for property."

Stevens smiled. For a second his eyes showed his disappointment. He recovered and went on. "I told Ronand..."

"It's Rónán"- he pronounced the name slowly so he would get it- "Mr. Stevens."

"Sorry. Your son needs a cosigner. He put down a nice down payment on a unit, but he is what, almost nineteen. I understand he is still in college. I explained it to him. He understands. So here I am."

So you can try to sell me a condo too.

"Did you bring a copy of the contract my son signed?"

"Yes. Of course," Stevens said, and pulled a sheaf of papers from his briefcase.

Donal took the papers with a business card attached and leafed through them. He paused at the back page. He kept his face unreadable as he set the paperwork aside.

"I'll have my attorney look through them. I'll get back with you later in the week."

"Very good," Stevens said as he gathered up his paperwork and stood, the meeting was over.

Martin joined Donal as soon as Stevens left. Donal filled him in on what was going on.

"Perhaps it is an investment," Martin said, as he glanced through the papers.

"I have a bad feeling about this," Donal said. "Take a look at the address on the last page."

"Oh," is all Martin said.

Tabitha announced that Pat Senior wanted to talk to him.

"I'll be right there." Then to Martin he said, "We'll talk about this later. After I talk to Rón."

Chapter Ten

If the condo was an investment, why hadn't Rón told him about it? As things turned out, Donal didn't get a chance to talk to his son that night.

Late the next afternoon, Donal was sitting in his office at Forest Lake going over the month's receipts. Martin had gone down to the stables. Donal planned to join him there later.

His work done, he turned his laptop off. The notes of "Carrighfergus" filled the air. He picked up his estate-linc and slid it open. It was Dominic Monaghan, their attorney. He worked for Donal and his partners, Mánus Scanlon and Liam O'Brien.

"How are you, Dominic?"

"Everything is fine here."

They talked about different things before Dominic came around to the reason he had called.

"How is Rónán doing?"

"He's doing well, spends most of his time studying. Do you want to speak to him? I don't think he is home yet."

"Donal..." Dominic paused, before he went on. "Skye informed me last week that Rónán is overdrawn on his allowance. Normally she just lets it go; things usually straighten out the next month. But he has been over-drawn for about six months. This morning he called. He asked to talk to me, not my daughter. He wanted to know if he could get an advance on another six months." Dominic's voice had a strange quality to it.

"What else, Dominic?"

"He also asked about the trust his mother set up for him. I reminded him that he can't draw on it until he turns twenty-five. At least not without your approval."

"Thanks, Dominic. I'll speak to him when he gets home later today. Tell Skye not to worry. It is probably nothing. Hold off on the advance on his allowance until I speak with him."

After Donal slid the phone closed, he pulled out the copy of the contract Walter Stevens had given him. He looked it over, noticing again the second address his son had given as a place to contact him at. It was an apartment in Prescott.

Donal hardly saw Rón during the week and only occasionally on weekends. He had thought that his son was studying at the campus library when not in class.

So what was he really doing?

He would have to face this straight on or take the chance of losing Rón. He picked up his estate-linc and entered Martin's number. When his foster son answered, he said, "We're going into town."

෴

Martin drove them out to the Stoney Brook apartment complex in Prescott. At 8976 Brook Park Dive, apartment #112A, he rang the doorbell. Donal said a silent prayer that this was a mistake, but in his heart, he knew his son was living here.

Almost as if they were expected, the door opened.

"Boy, that was fast...oh..." she stopped talking. Her blue eyes grew round, her face went white, and then her eyes narrowed in anger.

Donal recognized Jennifer, remembered seeing her sitting in the chapel the day he married Moya. She looked a lot like her mother, Barbara Strickland.

"Your son isn't here," Jennifer said, as she moved to close the door. Martin moved forward, stopping the door before she could close it. She frowned at him, then turned back to Donal. There was resentment in her eyes.

"May we come in?" Donal asked.

Somewhere in the back, a baby began to cry. Jennifer moved aside to let them enter. "Rón will be back soon. You can wait if you want. I need to see to my baby."

With a derisive gesture toward the couch, Jennifer left them standing in the living room. She disappeared down a short hall, and a minute later, a door closed.

Donal didn't sit down. He paced around the medium-sized apartment. He took in the used furniture, the wall mounted-video-screen across from the couch. He stepped into the small kitchen, with a round table for two, stove, refrigerator, and a few built-in cabinets.

He was angry, and confused. It wasn't hard to figure out what was going on here. Had Jennifer accused his son of being the father? Knowing his son, he would take on the responsibility for his child.

Martin put his hand on his arm. "Perhaps we should wait to see what is going on before we jump to any conclusions."

Donal sighed. Martin was right.

"If you're upset, Donal, think of how Strickland must feel. This isn't exactly sixteen Weathervane Lane."

Their apartment was neat and clean, but very blue-collar-nothing like the Strickland mansion, or Forest Lake for that matter. Why were they living here? Why had his son, his golden boy, taken up with the daughter of his enemy? Had she trapped him into marriage by getting pregnant? He suspected that if Strickland knew about the baby, he had thrown Jennifer out.

More important, was the baby his grandchild?

Donal sat down on the couch.

In the back room, the baby went on crying. Jennifer had put on a brave face, but she was upset, and the baby must have sensed it.

In the next apartment, someone banged on the wall, yelled, "Shut the goddamned baby up." Through the wall came the sound of the afternoon news as the volume was kicked up to drown out the crying.

He couldn't stand it any longer. The baby's hysterical cries wore him down. Donal stood and walked back to the bedroom. The door hadn't caught. It stood slightly ajar. Inside, Jennifer paced back and forth trying to soothe a tiny baby. She turned to face him as he pushed the door open. Her anger had been replaced with concern for her child.

"Let me see if I can help," he said holding out his hands to take the baby. "I could always soothe the boys."

Jennifer hesitated. "Rón can usually settle her down. I don't know what has gotten into her."

Did she know that he had been in love with her mother a long time ago? She frowned at Donal, and at Martin, who watched from the hall. She seemed to make up her mind and let Donal take the baby.

"What's your name, girseach?"

"Her name is Caitlín Aine. Please don't call her Cate-Lynn Ann."

Donal kissed the soft downy head. She smelled like a combination of talcum powder and formula. The smell brought back happy memories of his boys when they were babies.

Did Caitlín look like his son? She couldn't be more then a few weeks old. It was too soon to tell who she would look like. He lifted her and placed her against his shoulder, supporting her small head with his right hand. She sniffed several times, gurgled, and settled down. With sigh, she closed her eyes, content at last.

"How old is she?" Donal asked.

"Eight weeks next Tuesday."

Out in the hall the front doorbell rang several times. Jennifer went to answer it. Donal followed her out to the living room.

"Let Martin answer it."

She turned to Donal, puzzled.

"In case it's your neighbor."

Martin waited for the bell to ring again before he pulled the door open.

"Pizza for my...lady...oh..."

Rónán stood framed in the doorway, a large pizza box in one hand. When he recovered, he picked up the six-pack of pop from the ground.

Donal handed the baby back to Jennifer. "She should sleep now."

"I guess it is out in the open now," Rónán said.

After Rónán kissed Jennifer and his little girl, he went into the kitchen. The awkward silence in the living room was broken by the sound of the refrigerator door opening and banging closed. When he came out, Rónán asked, "Any one for pizza?"

Jennifer took the baby back to the bedroom. When she came out, she hugged Rón. They stood together holding hands to comfort each other.

Seeing them holding hands reminded Donal of Cynthia and himself. It seemed like a lifetime ago.

"Have a seat, Da, Martin," Rónán said as if this was an expected visit.

Donal sank down on the couch. Martin sat down next to him. Rónán brought chairs from the kitchen for Jennifer and himself to sit on.

"You know who I am?" Jennifer asked.

"Yes, of course I do," Donal answered.

"And you're not angry?"

"I'd have to be a saint not to be angry. To have this happen behind my back, with someone..." Donal was going to say, "outside our faith." He thought of himself as a Christian, but his faith was different than the way most people here believed.

"Da, it isn't what you think...We didn't have to get married. We wanted to."

Donal knew he was at a crossroads. One mistake now and he would lose his youngest son. He watched the young couple. Jennifer was a younger version of her mother. For an instant, there was a pang of regret, but it was gone in a heartbeat. Thinking about Barbara had brought back some bittersweet memories. Why couldn't she have stood up to her mother? But if she had, and had they married, what would have become of Moya?

He loved Moya with all his heart and being.

Perhaps Jennifer was different, stronger. She had married the man she loved. He stared down at his hands, tried to tell himself this was different. Was it? His son had the girl he loved. How could he find fault with that?

It wasn't going to be easy. Every time he looked at Jennifer, he would be reminded of who her father was. He would remember how Jason, her half brother, had attacked and maimed Robert, and threatened Donald.

On the other hand, perhaps this would put to rest the feud, bring the two families together. It was wishful thinking on his part. Nothing would change between Strickland and himself.

Rónán didn't say anything. He sat watching his father, waiting.

Donal wanted to get up and leave the apartment, not face this problem on top of everything else that was going on in his life. Like it or not, in his heart he knew he couldn't just leave. He had to face this.

Why had his son called Dominic about the trust in the first place? Asked for six months advance on his allowance when he was already overdrawn? The condo salesperson had told Rón that he would need a cosigner. It came to him in a flash, an epiphany. It was Rón's way of letting him know what was going on.

Donal had to think of the little girl in the next room, and his son, as well as Jennifer Strickland. He corrected himself, Jennifer Tolan.

"The marriage is legal," Jennifer said, as if she had misunderstood his silence.

"I never doubted it for a minute. Do you go by Jennifer?"

"No, Jenny."

"We were married during spring break, as soon as we were old enough to not need someone to sign for us," Rónán added. "I suppose you could try to have it annulled because of our age."

Donal made up his mind. Hard as it was he had to accept his new daughter-in-law. But then, life was never easy.

"I would never try to have it annulled," he said, and smiled at them, a real smile. "Sally Brown and Mrs. Murphy will feel slighted if you don't come to Forest Lake for a reception and the clan blessing. I'm sure the Ladies will be happy to make, or help you with, arrangements." He paused, "Or if not at Forest Lake, anywhere you want."

Jennifer turned to her young husband. He smiled at her, squeezed her hand, and nodded.

"Rón said you would understand. I didn't believe him, not for a minute. I begged him not to tell you.

I'll be honest, I didn't think you would be any different than my father."

"Does he know about the baby?"

"Not yet. He cut me off when he learned who I was dating."

There was still doubt in her eyes. He would have to work hard to make friends with her, to prove that all the things her father had told her weren't true.

Donal made another decision.

"Your condo is well away from town."

Well away from Forest Lake too. If Fountain Park was associated with the new mall, he didn't want anything to do with it. He would also like to see his son living on this side of the Prescott River. "I am sure you could get your deposit back. If not, I am sure Dominic could help if they refuse. There are some nice homes up near Weathervane Lane. Jenny and the baby would be close to her family."

"We are on a month-by-month arrangement here...I was...well now that you know I..." Rónán said. As if she knew what her husband was going to say, Jenny stiffened at his side. He gave her hand another squeeze. "If we could...if we could come home. We can think about a house later."

Donal smiled. "It isn't as if you really ever left, Rón. Your room is big enough for two."

"My room would be fine. Would Saturday be too soon?"

"When you are ready, give us a call."

Donal looked over at Martin. His Guardian knew that he was very happy.

Martin stood. "I'll just step outside and give Mrs. Murphy a heads-up on what is going on. So they can freshen up your room, Rón."

"Ask Carl to bring down the cradle from storage in the attic," Donal said, before Martin stepped outside.

Donal turned to his son and daughter-in-law. "It will need a new mattress. It was a gift from the O'Briens when Rón was born. He grew so fast he didn't use it long."

Father and son stood and hugged. Then Donal hugged Jenny. She held herself stiff, but perhaps one day they would become friends.

"How about pizza, Da?"

Pizza wasn't one of his favorite things to eat. But at that moment, Donal would eat anything. "Sounds good to me."

Months later, this afternoon would come back to haunt Donal. He would wonder how he had miscalculated how strong Jenny Strickland seemed on that day. But at that moment, he was too happy to think about anything else. His son was bringing his wife and child home to Forest Lake. He would remind himself that you can't see all the paths you could take in life. No one could. Not even Brid could see all of them.

CHAPTER ELEVEN

When Donal received the second letter, he knew he had missed something important. On his office laptop, he pulled up the menu for the camera room on the third floor. He never used the cameras in his office. But something kept nagging at the edge of his thoughts.

What had he missed?

From the menu, he programmed the camera by the front windows facing the living room section into his office, and the camera above the sword case, to come on anytime someone entered the office.

He was about to turn the computer off, thought better of it, and for some unknown reason, but one he was sure was valid, he turned on the camera on the first level of the studio building, even though it hadn't been used since Cynthia's death.

Then he called Seán Scanlon, something he had been putting off. Seán came on the line. "MSS, Seán speaking."

"Seán, I was wondering if you could give me a little information."

"What can I help you with, Donal?"

"Alvin, is he a loner, or does he hang out with any-one in particular?"

"That's easy. He hangs out with Michael O."

Michael O was one of Liam's grandsons.

Whether he liked it or not, he was called Michael O so he wasn't confused with Michael Scanlon. Alvin and Michael O. That explained a lot of things.

"Your father had you do a check on the Ryan clan a while back. Could you do a check for me?"

"Of course, Donal. The Ryans again?"

"No, check into Michael O."

"Done. I'll call you back as soon as I have all the information."

Donal had half expected Seán to be surprised at his request. He stood and walked over to the bar to make more tea, found the canister almost empty. Donal had learned some time ago to make his own tea rather than bother either of the Ladies. He walked down the hall to the kitchen to get a new canister.

Jenny sat at the huge old-fashioned wooden kitchen table, helping mix dough to make scones, with Sally Brown. When Donal entered the room, she looked up. She looked down so quickly she almost dumped the dough into her lap. She kept her head down as she worked the dough.

With Jenny, it was hard to tell if her reaction was fear or disgust, most likely disgust toward him.

Later, Sally Brown brought a plate of warm scones to his office. She set the plate on his desk.

"Be patient," Sally Brown said. "It will take a while before she comes around."

"Thank you," Donal said, reaching for a scone. "And for drawing her into the workings of the house."

"I don't think at this point she knows what to think about you, or any of us, for that matter. She is quiet most of the time. I worry about her. The one good thing is she has hit if off with Moya."

Perhaps, Donal thought, he should bring up Jenny's quietness with Rón. No, he would wait to see if his son would bring up the subject.

❧

A week later, Donal was down in the first stable checking Ghost Warrior. They would be putting him out in the north pasture soon with a dozen mares. After washing up, he walked out the side door. At the end corral, Jenny stood by the fence watching Cinnamon, a small young filly that the Humane Society had asked him to board until they found her a permanent home.

Jenny didn't know the slightest thing about horses. Each time she reached to pat the filly, she moved too fast. Scared, the filly would back away. He was tempted to go over and help her, but knew she would only take offense.

He walked back to the stable office.

Carl was working on the computer. Alvin was lounging on the folding chair against the wall. When he saw Donal, he stood up and acted as if he was getting instruction from Carl.

"I need to talk to Carl," Donal said.

After Alvin left, Donal closed the door.

"How are things working out with Alvin?"

"Not too bad, and not too good. He does just enough to get by," Carl said.

"Actually," Donal said, sitting down on the folding chair, "I was wondering if Jenny comes down here often?"

"She likes Cinnamon, comes down at least once a day. Donal, are you thinking of keeping the filly?"

"No. But if Jenny likes her, I might be persuaded to change my mind."

"Good luck with her. She is even quieter than Cathal O'Brien, Alvin's father."

Donal agreed and went back up to the house.

CHAPTER TWELVE

Donal very seldom had days off. There was always something to do around the farm, at O'Flaherty's, or he had to go up to Chicago to MSS. But when he did, he liked to spend the time with Moya. She kept to their third-floor apartment, only coming down for meals when he was home.

Today was one of those days when he had the whole afternoon off. When he didn't find Moya in the solarium at lunchtime, he went up to their apartment. He was surprised to find Jenny with her.

For some reason, Moya wasn't speaking English, and Jenny didn't speak Irish, yet they seemed to be getting along fine. He paused in the doorway, watching them. Moya loved children, had helped Mór with the many children at Faolán.

Jenny was feeding Caitlín. "I am going to ask Fionn to help me with my Irish."

Moya looked up and smiled at Donal. "Please join us, mo ghrá."

Jenny glanced up, looking disappointed to see him. "I had better be going," she said, standing.

"Please stay for lunch," Donal said. "How is Caitlín doing today?"

"She is fine," Jenny said. She hesitated before sitting down again.

The once friendly-room now seemed cold and the conversation forced. Donal noted the confusion on Moya's face, as she looked from Jenny to him. He was relieved when the lunch was brought in.

After lunch, Donal loaded up a tray and took the dishes down to the kitchen. When he got back upstairs, Jenny and Caitlín were gone.

Moya said, "What is it between you two?"

"Jenny doesn't like me."

"That is hard to believe. She is the daughter of your heart, and you show nothing but kindness to her."

"She thinks I am the Fear Dubh."

"Fear Dubh? Surely you jest."

"No, grá." He held his index fingers along each side of his head. Moya giggled. But then grew serious. From her expression he knew she didn't understand why he would make horns on his head. "Her father is my enemy. She believes what he told her."

"She will learn what a good person you are."

"I have the afternoon off. What would you like to do? We could go riding, watch a movie, or go into town."

Moya smiled at him. "Anything?"

"Yes, anything you wish."

Moya stood and took him by the hand. He was surprised when she didn't head toward the stairs. Instead, she led him back to their bedroom.

Donal pulled out his estate-linc and keyed in "Emergency Calls Only," set it down on the dresser, and closed the door behind them.

CHAPTER THIRTEEN

It was time to decide what to do with Cinnamon. Donal would have to call the Humane Society soon.

They were having dinner when he casually said, "I am going to call the Humane Society and tell them they need to find a home for the filly."

"I thought you were thinking of keeping her," Rónán said.

"Is there a problem?" Moya asked. Her English had improved, but sometimes she still had trouble following a conversation.

Donal explained to her in Irish what they were talking about.

"Carl doesn't have time to train her to a bridle and saddle." He never called it breaking, he called it training a horse.

Jenny watched him, but didn't comment. She didn't speak much during their meals together. Donal was sure that she was more open when she was alone with Rón, as she was with Moya.

The subject was dropped. Donal decided to wait and see what would happen. He didn't have long to wait. The next morning, Jenny came to his office. She knocked and walked in without waiting to be asked to come in.

Donal stood up, Martin, who was sitting in one of the chairs in front of the desk, stood also.

"Jenny," Martin said, turned back to Donal, "I'll check with Seán and talk to you later."

When they were alone, Jenny said, "I was wondering about Cinnamon."

Donal motioned for her to join him in the living room part of his office. "Can I get you something? Tea, coffee, a glass of water?"

Jenny said, "I'm fine." She walked over to the glass case. "Are these things you have collected?"

"No, they are things that belonged to my ancestors."

Jenny glanced at the chess game set up on the end of the coffee table. "Rón has tried to teach me how to play," she said and sat down at the other end of the couch closest to the door. Donal moved to that end and sat down across from her. "What do you want to know about Cinnamon?"

"You could train her, right?"

"Yes, I could. But she needs someone to take care of her after that. Someone that will ride her, see to her needs, see that she gets enough exercise. Much like Martin and I take care of our horses. Carl is too busy..." He stopped, waited.

Her eyes told him she was having trouble making up her mind. "She isn't going to get much bigger, is she?"

"No, she is a small horse, but not quite as small as a pony," Donal answered.

"I'll take care of her. I don't ride, but perhaps when Caitlín is old enough to learn to ride, she could start with Cinnamon."

Donal didn't want to sound too agreeable, so again he waited.

"Honest, I'll take care of her."

"Okay," Donal said, as if making up his mind. "We'll start tomorrow, right after you put Caitlín down for her afternoon nap."

As soon as Jenny left, Donal called the Humane Society and let them know he would keep Cinnamon. They were pleased at the news and admitted they were having trouble finding a new home for her.

Chapter Fourteen

The next afternoon, Jenny was waiting for Donal down at the first corral, where Carl had moved Cinnamon. He was pleased to see she had put on a long-sleeved shirt and a pair of old jeans.

"Do you want a hat?" he asked.

"I don't own one."

Donal went into the first stable and back to the tack room. On the top shelf, he found a wide-brimmed hat that Rón used to wear. He presented it to Jenny, letting her know it was Rón's hat.

She put it on and gave him a nervous smile. "I probably look silly."

"You look fine," he said, keeping his voice soft and reassuring. "I want you to work with me as much as possible once Cinnamon gets used to being handled. I want her to know she belongs to you."

They would start with making friends with the filly. Donal put two carrots in his back pocket and entered the corral. Cinnamon ran to the back, looking for a way out. She turned left and ran along the fence. He waited at the center, until she settled down.

"Good luck." Carl said as he came over to stand next to Jenny.

"Will this take long?" she asked.

"Donal will have her eating out of his hand in a couple of days."

Donal turned away from Carl and Jenny, his full attention on Cinnamon.

Cinnamon backed into the left-hand corner, watchful. Donal held out a carrot to her. He didn't move. He let her smell the offering. He was pleased when her nose quivered and she moved closer. She took a few steps closer, then stretched out her neck toward him. Donal let her take the carrot, greens and all. He waited until she finished the first carrot before he offered her the second one.

This time she stepped closer.

Donal let her take the second carrot, then turned and walked back to the gate. Outside, he went over with Jenny how much to feed the filly, and to make sure her water trough was full.

"Tomorrow, I want you to offer her a carrot."

"She won't bite me, will she?"

"Not if you are careful."

At the end of a month, Donal was pleased to find that Jenny had come to an understanding with him. If they were not friends, at least they were on better terms than before. Working together with Cinnamon, they both seemed to forget their differences. Jenny was still quiet at meals, but she seemed more relaxed.

CHAPTER FIFTEEN

Rónán joined Donal down at the corral to watch Jenny work with Cinnamon. She placed the bridle over Cinnamon's head, checked the buckle, and moved over to place the saddle blanket on her back. When she had the saddle on and the girth tightened, she walked the filly around the corral.

"I must be imaging things," Rónán said. "I had the feeling last week I was followed into town, and again today. I swear I saw the same car I saw earlier in the week."

"It is a small town, probably just someone who lives in the area," Donal said. Rón was a very observant person. It had to be true. He wouldn't say anything until he knew for sure. Later he would call Seán Scanlon.

Jenny waved and smiled at them, then pulled her hat off and bowed. At the same time, she pulled on the bridle, and Cinnamon bowed with her.

Rónán and Donal applauded her.

"Thanks, Da."

Donal turned to his son and smiled. "She did most of it on her own."

"You know what I mean. She is so quiet sometimes. I worry about her. I haven't seen her happier since Caitlín was born."

"Is there something you want to talk to me about, Rón?"

As Rónán watched Jenny, Donal watched him. Rónán didn't speak right away. When he did, he said, "No, no. She just gets into these moods sometimes."

Donal hoped he would say more, but Rón chose not to.

ᕦᕤ

Jenny laid the plastic sheet over the blue-and-gold duvet. She didn't like using the changing table in the corner. Once that was done, she laid Caitlín on top. As she changed her little girl, Rónán came into their bedroom.

"My two girls," he said with a smile and sat down next to his daughter. Caitlín kicked her legs and waved her arms around, gurgled, and smiled, almost, but not quite, managing to roll over.

"As soon as I get her down for her nap, I am going down to see to Cinnamon. Do you have time?"

"It's Saturday. I have all the time in the world. I'd love to go down with you," he said.

"Perhaps later, Alvin will make tea for us."

"Tea?"

"Yes. He makes tea for me all the time."

Rónán frowned at her.

"No long faces today, please," she said. "He isn't as bad as I was led to believe."

Rónán smiled at her. "I guess he has mellowed out being here at Forest Lake."

"I find it peaceful here too. I just wish we had more room for Caitlín's things," Jenny said. "All the gifts are still packed in boxes and piled in the closet." She picked up a box from the nightstand and opened the silver tissue paper, pulled out a tiny linen dress with lace on the sleeves and hem. She held it out for Rón to see.

"Look at this. Isn't it lovely? It is from the Hewson family in Ireland."

Rónán glanced at the dress, then returned to studying the wall by the bed.

"Something wrong?"

"Let me take our little princess." He stood and picked up his daughter. "Now come with me."

Jenny was surpised when they didn't head toward the stairs. Instead, they turned right. At the next room, Rón opened the door, flicked on the light, and let her go in first.

Jenny looked around the room.

All the furniture had heavy cloth covers on to protect it from dust. The room had a heavy closed-in smell.

"Was this Robert's or Donald's room?" she asked.

"No, it is the room that Martin used when he first came to live with us. He now has a room in the west wing." Rónán addressed Caitlín. "How would you like a room of your own, Cat?"

"You're kidding, Rón."

"No. All we have to do is make a door between our room and this one. It would give our princess a room for all her things."

"That would be wonderful," Jenny said. "Will he let us do that?"

"Donal loves Caitlín. I am sure he would agree we need more space." Rónán paused. "Do you like my father?"

"Of course I do."

"Really?"

Jenny walked to the windows, pulled back the drapes, and looked out. The view was no different than the one from their room.

She turned and said, "I respect him. He is a hard worker." She smiled at Rón. "He gave me Cinnamon, and I will forever be grateful. My father didn't allow pets of any kind in our home or on the property. I missed that growing up."

"Well, Cat, I think it is settled."

Jenny shook her head in mock exasperation.

"Are you really going to call her Cat?"

"Everyone gets a nickname. If you mind, I'll stop."

Rónán patted Caitlín's back as he did a slow dance around the room, singing a song in English to her. Jenny loved watching Rón with their little girl.

When Caitlín lowered her head to his shoulder, Rónán said, "Let's take her down and place her in the bed downstairs. One of the Ladies will be happy to watch her."

"Why are you singing to her in English?" Jenny asked as they walked into the hall.

"She learns English first. Later, if she wants, I can teach her Irish. Besides, the Ladies don't speak Irish well."

Jenny was happy about the new room, a real nursery for their daughter. She followed Rón down the stairs. She paused for a second on the landing. Lately she wasn't feeling well. Could she be pregnant again?

CHAPTER SIXTEEN

Donal and Martin were just getting back from the east pasture. With Carl and Alvin's help, they brought in a dozen horses, many of which would be taken to the autumn horse auction south of Terra Haute.

When the notes of "Carrighfergus" filled the air, Donal pulled out his estate-linc. He slid back the top, smiled, and took the call.

It was Mark Sims, the sheriff for Prescott County.

"Donal here." As Donal listened, his smile faded, and a frown replaced it. "Give us an hour. We just came in from the east pasture." He listened again. "No problem, bring him over. The gate will be open."

He closed the estate-linc.

"What's wrong?" Martin asked.

"Joseph Strickland thinks we are holding his sister here against her will. Mark Sims is coming out with him." Donal keyed in Rón's number into his estate-linc, waited, then said, "Are you still at the library? Can you come home? Your brother-in-law is coming over."

He filled Rón in on what was going on. Up at the main house, he told Sally Brown and Mrs. Murphy to expect guests.

After washing up, Donal joined Martin and his family down in the solarium. Moya and Jenny sat at the table with cups of tea. Rónán was holding his daughter. He paced back and forth in front of the floor-to-ceiling windows. He was upset by the accusation.

An hour later, almost to the minute, the doorbell rang. The voices out in the hall carried back to the solarium.

"Jenny! Where are you?"

Mrs. Murphy escorted Joseph Strickland and Mark Sims back to the solarium. As soon as Joseph saw his sister, he hurried over to her.

"I've come to get you. I have the sheriff with me. They can't hold you here against your will."

Jenny gave him a puzzled look. "What are you talking about, Joseph? Rón and I are married."

"What!" Joseph said, puzzled. He turned to Donal. "I would like to speak to my sister in private."

Donal turned to his son. Rón nodded.

Moya stood, taking Donal's lead, she followed the men into living room. Joseph closed the French doors behind them so that Jenny and he could talk in private.

"I know you are on duty, Mark. Can I get you some coffee or tea? Perhaps one of Sally's famous scones to go with it?"

"Thank you for the offer. I'll just wait here for Joseph. I don't think this will take long."

"You know the marriage is legal," Rónán said to Mark as he escorted Moya to a couch and let her take Caitlín.

"I know that, but Strickland is behind this, so I agreed to accompany Joseph out here. To make sure nothing gets out of hand."

Mrs. Murphy entered and announced, "There is coffee, tea, small sandwiches, and scones in the dining room."

"Mark, this might take some time after all. Let's go into the dining room for at least a cup of coffee," Donal said.

In the dining room, Donal let Mark help himself to coffee from the decanter on the sideboard. He also encouraged him to have something to eat.

Mark took his cup of coffee and stepped over to the oak breakfront. "That is an interesting design with the two crossed flags on the serving plate." He glanced at the plates and cups. "Is that an oak leaf on one and a horse on the other flag?"

"Yes, they are my family standards. Cynthia Long designed the pattern and had Royal Tara in Galway, Ireland make the china for us."

"It's beautiful," Mark said as he took a plate from the long sideboard and helped himself to a sandwich and several scones. "You don't see fancy china with gold rims as much as you used to." He sat down at the oak dining room table that could seat a dozen people without adding the two leaves.

Rónán served himself a cup of tea and waited by the front windows. Moya sat with Caitlín in her usual place to the right of the head of the table. Martin positioned himself so he could watch the hall and French doors to the living room.

Donal sat down next to Martin. This was his son's fight. They were here for back up. It wasn't likely that Joseph would try anything with Mark here, but Donal wasn't taking any chances.

They waited over an hour before Jenny walked her brother out into the hall. They stood facing each other. From their size and coloring, they could be mistaken for twins, there was love there too. They hugged, turned and hand in hand walked into the dining room.

"I want to thank you for being so understanding and letting me come out here on such short notice," Joseph said. "My father led me to believe that you were holding Jenny against her will."

Rónán put down his teacup and held out his hand to his brother-in-law. "You don't have to worry about Jenny."

"I know that now."

Donal stepped forward to shake hands with Joseph. "Come visit anytime you want to."

"Enough. Joseph, come and meet your niece, Caitlín Aine," Jenny said as she pulled him over to where Moya sat holding her little girl. Joseph picked her up. Caitlín Aine looked at him with her large hazel eyes, smiled, and gave his beard a tentative pull, then with both hands grabbed harder.

"Ouch," Joseph said. "She has quite a grip." He handed her back to Moya. "She is beautiful."

"I have something else to show you." Jenny turned to Donal. "May I take him below?"

"Of course, Jenny," Donal said.

When they were alone, Mark said, "He'll go back to San Francisco reassured that his sister is fine."

Late that night, up on the top floor of the studio building at Forest Lake, in what had been Cynthia and Donal's original apartment, as well as her studio, Alvin O'Brien sat at the kitchen table. He glanced at his watch. It was after midnight. Even Carl was in bed by now.

With care, he took apart several tea bags. He dumped the contents into a bowl. Then he added a concoction that he'd received from a close friend. To this mix he added several chemicals he had saved for this day.

He mixed the dry ingredients together, sniffed at the bowl, and decided that he needed more tea. After adding more tea and mixing it again, he carefully refilled the tea bags and stapled them closed. He was careful that each bag he filled wouldn't look any different than the other bags in the box.

When he was done, he closed the box of tea bags. He placed his supplies into a shoebox and hid it in the bottom drawer in the end kitchen cabinet.

From the same drawer, he took out a brown cardboard box with holes in the lid and a rock on top to keep it in place. Inside, a small dead mouse lay.

"Well, so it works." He smiled to himself. "This batch I made just a little stronger. I need a bigger animal to try it on."

He smiled while he scraped out the remaining concoction into a paper bag. He would throw this into the trash. Fionn's rabbit would work fine for his next experiment.

It was time he taught them all a lesson, including Mánus Scanlon.

CHAPTER SEVENTEEN

Donal received a third letter. It was time to talk to Brid again. Their talk earlier in the summer hadn't explained the dream, not to Donal's satisfaction.

The letters were a problem he needed resolved before he returned to Cwillan to get Devlin. He called Brid, and they agreed to meet later in the week.

Rónán and Jenny planned to come with Donal and Martin for a mini vacation on Lake Michigan. At the last moment, Jenny became ill and decided to stay home. She told Rónán to go. She didn't mind being alone since they would be gone only a few days. Besides, she reminded him, she had Caitlín and Moya and the Ladies to keep her company.

Before Donal and Martin drove to Michigan City to see Brid, Donal reminded Carl that Alvin was not to go into town alone. He also called St. Anthony's, asked them to keep Johnnie Coffey and Siobhán Dunn on until the end of the year. Donal didn't expect them to say no. O'Flaherty's was one of their biggest contributors.

Martin knocked on the door. They didn't have long to wait. The door flew open, and Rhyianna stood before them. On seeing Donal, a big smile lit up her pretty young face. With a squeal of delight, she stepped forward, on tiptoes, reached up, and hugged Donal. Then, in a more sedate manner, she hugged Martin.

She called over her shoulder, "Mother, we have company."

Brid came out into the hall. "Well don't leave them out there on the porch."

"I'll be in the kitchen if you need me," Martin said.

"Are you okay? You look a little pale," Donal asked.

"I probably ate too much last night," Martin said and headed toward the kitchen.

Donal thought it strange that first Jenny came down with something, now Martin didn't look well. He hoped the flu wasn't going around.

Brid led him into the living room.

Her house on Greenwood Avenue was over two hundred years old. The living room had a fireplace that dominated the middle of the wall, across from the hall entrance, with small windows set high on each side. There were tall windows to the left that looked out onto the front porch and lawn. To the right, at the end of the oblong room, French doors opened onto a sun-porch with tall windows on three sides.

Brid motioned for Donal to have a seat in one of the huge stuffed chairs that flanked the fireplace.

Donal loved the feel to this room, nice and comfortable. Brid had lived here for several years. On warm evenings, Tómas and Brid drove down to Lake Michigan and walked out to the old lighthouse. Donal had offered to get them a boat, but neither Tomás nor Brid seemed interested in going out onto the lake.

"Rhya, please make some tea for our guests."

Brid closed the French doors to the hall and moved over to sit on the couch across from Donal.

"Rhyianna is growing up to be a beautiful young lady," Donal said.

"She has a terrible crush on you."

"She'll grow out of it."

"I wonder if she will," Brid said. "You have enchanted many women."

Embarrassed, Donal said, "I think you have me mistaken with Mánus."

Brid took out her cards and put down a row of seven cards face-up. "I see an Asian lady who cares for you."

Lily Cheng came to mind. Donal was surprised. "I thought Lily was interested in one of my sons. I guess I never gave it much thought. Her father is very old-fashioned and will have her marry someone from their community." Uncomfortable with the subject, he decided to change it and said, "Does Rhyianna know who her father is?"

"Tomás is her father. That is all she needs to know."

"Moya would love to have a child."

"She needs to be patient." Brid smiled at Donal. "Rhya has inherited her father's intelligence." She placed seven more cards face-up. "He is a gentleman and will never tell." Brid gave Donal a meaningful look. "So what brings you all the way out here?"

"Some strange things have been going on. Perhaps you can clarify them for me?"

"Still worried about the dream?" Brid asked.

"It was so vivid, it would be hard to forget."

"You are looking good," she said. "Keeping fit."

"For my age," he added.

"Your age," Brid laughed. "Interesting, you were the youngest of the Four Horsemen. I think your father and uncle lied about your age to make it easier for the chieftains to accept you as the heir to the throne. I doubt that you know what your true age is. And your ID..."

Brid stopped as the French doors opened and Tomás brought in a tray with tea things on it. He set the tray at the end of the coffee table to the left of his wife. Rhyianna followed him in.

"Thank you, Tomás." And to her daughter she said, "It looks good."

Most Americans just dropped a tea bag into hot water, not giving any thought to what it would taste like. In Ireland and in many Irish-American homes, making tea was an art passed down from mother to daughter. Brid had passed on the art to her only child, Rhyianna.

When they were alone again, Brid said, "You have the heart of a warrior. Your son has the heart of a lion."

"Rónán?"

Brid looked up from her cards. "No, the dark one."

"Feargus?" The horrible dream flashed in his mind again. He forced it out of his thoughts so his full attention was on Brid.

"Would you go back to help him? Would you become a warrior again?"

Donal hesitated. He didn't know why. "I doubt he would ask for my help." He frowned at Brid. "Will I have to?"

"I know so little about him. His future is not clear. But yours has many paths, and one might be to help Feargus. But that is not why you came here. Trying to help you find someone is out of my expertise."

Donal smiled. "You are always a step ahead of me. Will we catch the man writing the letters?"

Brid made another row of seven cards on the coffee table.

"He was taught well. Therefore, he will be hard to catch." Brid started a fourth row of seven cards. "In the end, you are smarter than he is. It is confusing, but one that cares for him will help you. Dealing with kin is a hard thing. As you well know."

Surprised at her words, he said, "Yes, it isn't an easy thing to do." Thoughts of his cousin Artúr came to mind. Dealing with kin was a very hard thing to do.

"You are worried about something else." It was a statement, not a question. "Did you bring me something of yours?"

Donal stood and pulled the pouch that held his talisman from his jacket pocket. He handed it to Brid and went to the tray and served the tea, added two teaspoons of sugar to each cup, then a third to one cup. He placed the cup with extra sugar close to Brid, and took his over to the chair and placed it on the end table.

Brid started a fifth row of cards, then a sixth. She sat staring at the cards with the fingers of her right hand on the pouch. She looked up at Donal and said, "You can still wield your broadsword."

Donal had wanted to ask why she seemed concerned about his age and his health. He knew the reason now. He might have to go back and fight again. Sometimes talking to Brid, you thought she had gone in a different direction, only to find you were exactly where she wanted to go.

"Yes. Martin makes a good sparring partner," he said.

"You work both right-and-left handed?"

"Yes. Niall wanted me to learn in this manner, and my father agreed that it makes better balance. According to historians, Brian Mór's oldest son fought with a sword in either hand, some claim one in each hand."

"Your house is very valuable."

Surprised again, Donal sat forward, his tea, the pleasant surroundings forgotten. "Rón dreamed one night that our house burned down. Is it some sort of premonition?"

Brid placed another card on the table, stopped as if she was reading something before her.

"The paintings in my house are lithographs of Cynthia's original work." Donal reached for his tea, then stopped. "All that is of value in the house, of material things, is my broadsword, a few relics I found in the Great Desert, and an old book." His tea forgotten again, he asked, "Will the house burn down? Rón said in the dream he was out on the front lawn, watching while the flames consumed the house, going higher and higher, toward the third floor."

Brid stared at the cards, tapping her finger on the table.

"Should he have come instead of me? He is over at Askeaton. Cathal could drive him over."

"No, your coming is more important, since it seems to involve you. Your apartment is on the third floor?"

"Yes."

Brid sighed. "Something is going to happen. The house may symbolize something else. Something terrible, something..." Brid paused and placed two more cards on the table. "It might be good to have your broadsword copied, and the book." Brid took a sip of her tea. "You remembered I have a sweet tooth," she said. "But that is still not all that you came here about."

"Someone is haunting me. Has been for a while."

Brid looked down at the cards, dealt out three more.

"Someone dead, perhaps someone you killed, or you wouldn't say he is haunting you."

Donal smelled again the acrid, sickening scent of burning flesh from down the years, during the war with the north. Brid's voice cut though to him.

"Don't think about it. It will only cloud things, make it harder for me to see, to help you." She paused, before she said, "It must be strange to live in two worlds. Two different men in one body, so to speak. One that many would mistake for a barbarian, and the other a smooth businessman and horse breeder."

Donal waited.

"Your life, in the other world is not over or, should I say, will never be finished. I think you will always return to the place of your birth. Your son...yes, it involves your dark son...or perhaps one of the other dark ones..."

"You don't mean one of the twins, Robert or Donald?"

Before she could go on, Donal's estate-linc went off, filling the room with the notes of "Carrighfergus." Donal pulled it out, slid it open, and glanced at the caller ID. "I have to take this. It might be about my daughter-in-law." He stood to go back to the sun-porch to take the call.

"I'll just step out in the hall..." Brid stopped.

They faced each other across the room. His heart went cold at the look on her face.

"I'm so sorry," she whispered.

Donal almost dropped the estate-linc. Finally he remembered that Seán was waiting for him.

"Donal here."

He listened to Seán, sat down before his legs gave out. His hand trembled so badly he dropped the estate-linc. Leaving it to lay on the carpet, he buried his face in his hands.

In the hall, Brid was calling for Martin.

The next thing he heard was, "This is Martin. Yes. I'll drive him back to Askeaton." He closed the estate-linc and slipped it into Donal's pocket. "When you are ready, I'll drive you back. They'll wait until you get there."

CHAPTER EIGHTEEN

Rónán Tolan and Mary Rose Scanlon, Mánus's oldest daughter, sat at the grand piano in the study at Askeaton.

Mary Rose hummed a few bars of a song.

"I know that one," Rónán said as he played the notes on the piano.

"That is amazing," she cried.

"Not really, I have perfect pitch, and a good memory helps."

Mary Rose hummed another song, an older one.

Rónán hesitated only a second before he played the notes.

"How is Martin doing?" Mary Rose asked. She was never subtle when it came to Martin.

Rónán smiled and continued playing the next verse of the song.

Sooner or later Mary Rose would get around to talking about Martin Rinn, his father's Guardian. Unfortunately for her, he didn't think that Mánus would ever consider Martin as a son-in-law.

Rónán didn't want to guess songs or talk about Martin. He wanted to get home. The news they received earlier that Jenny had gone to the Prescott post office and failed to meet Carl later at O'Flaherty's had him upset.

Donal had wanted to go straight home, but Rónán had convinced his father to see Brid first. After that, they would drive home.

Jamie Ryan, Thomas Lynch, and Sheriff Sims were looking for Jenny.

Mary Rose asked again, "How is Martin doing?"

"Sorry. You know, quiet," Rónán said.

"Is there anyone he is interested in?"

Out in the hall, the front door opened and closed. The sound of hushed voices filtered into the study.

"Looks like your father is back..."

Rónán glanced up, wondering why Mary Rose had stopped talking. He turned to see what she was looking at. Donal and Mánus were standing side by side just inside the sliding doors.

"Mary Rose, dear, please, I need to talk to you," Mánus said.

She stood and joined her father. He put his arm around her, and together they turned and walked into the hall. Martin stepped forward and pulled the sliding doors closed.

Rónán turned around, so he was now sitting with his back to the piano. His father stood near the door, his head down, not moving into the room. A cold lump grew in the pit of his stomach. Something had happened, something bad. *Please, God,* Rónán prayed, *don't let it be Jenny or my little girl.*

As if finally making up his mind, Donal walked over to the bar. He stood scanning the bottles for what he wanted. He took down a bottle of Screech and poured out a generous portion into a tumbler. He brought it back to his son.

"Before we go, there is something I need to tell you," Donal said, handing the glass toward his son.

Rónán refused it.

Donal gulped the fiery rum down in one swallow.

Everyone gathered out in the hall heard the scream.

Mánus put his arm around his daughter, feeling the pain he heard in Rónán's voice. Mánus keyed in Seán's number. When his son answered, he said, "Call Keith Little. Find out what happened at the post office."

CHAPTER NINETEEN

Joseph Strickland broke down in tears before finishing the eulogy for his sister. A friend helped the sobbing young man to his seat. Father Victor Tanner stood and turned to face the mourners.

Father Tanner, a member, of the New Catholic Church, led them in a prayer for the repose of the soul of Jennifer Strickland Tolan. The service was similar to what the Catholic Church would have had, but different in some ways.

When it was over, he said, "On behalf of the Tolan and Strickland families, I want to thank you for coming. There will be a brunch at Forest Lake. Everyone is invited. I have maps if you don't know the way from here."

Mánus Scanlon stood and walked over to Moya to escort her back to her car. She was dressed in a black mourning dress, with a black silk veil over her hair. Many of the people assembled for the funeral were dressed in black. The rest of the Scanlon and O'Brien clan followed them down the hill.

In the back Johnnie Coffey stood, in a new navy suit, bought just for the funeral. He began to play "Lament for Frankie," one of Jenny's favorites. It was a lovely piece, but Donal wished his son had picked less somber music. Alvin and Michael O sat at the back. Were they talking, or scheming?

Donal moved out from under the canopy. The day was hot with a cloudless blue sky above. He moved over to stand at the foot of Cynthia Tolan's grave. In Irish he said, "I'm sorry, Cyn. I failed our son. If only we had stayed home. Dear Father, please forgive me." He touched his forehead, then his chest.

"What will it take to get you to join my flock?" Victor Tanner asked.

"I wasn't raised a Catholic, Father." *At least not the modern church dogma,* Donal added to himself.

"I suppose I will have to be content that at least you believe. So many don't these days."

Victor Tanner had come today because Donal was a good friend of Jonathan Turner, in a way Victor's boss.

"I don't know which is worse, burying someone on a beautiful day like today, or when it is cold and rainy."

No day was good for burying a loved one, Donal thought.

Donal thanked Victor Tanner for the service, made sure he was coming to the house, then moved back under the canopy. He pulled at his collar. He hated ties. He often wondered who had invented them, and why? It made a good way to catch a man in a fight.

O'Flaherty's was closed for the funeral. The servers, busboys and kitchen staff attending the service were dressed in navies and blacks. They filed by Donal, giving him their condolences. He thanked each one for coming and gave each one a personal invitation to Forest Lake.

Barbara Strickland joined him. They hugged, each feeling the other's pain.

"I won't be coming to the house."

"I understand," Donal said.

Behind them, Terrence Strickland said, "Let's go, Barbara." He started down the hill, stopped, and turned back to Donal. "My lawyer will get in touch with you about my grandchild, Caitlín Aine." He pronounced her name as "Cate-Lynn Ann."

"Don't bother, Strickland. You don't want anyone to find out about what you did at the post office. We have it on video from a surveillance camera across the street."

Strickland's eyes narrowed as he scowled at Donal.

They didn't really have anything on tape, but Strickland didn't know that. All they had was a witness coming out of the post office. Neither Seán nor KC Little had found a link between Strickland and Sundance Enterprise.

Making a guess, Donal said, "Of course, there is also what people would think if they found out you are the one behind the new mall."

Strickland looked as if he was going to have a stroke. His face went crimson, and he tried to speak. Failing that, he turned and hurried down the hill, forcing Barbara to hurry to keep up.

The sound of subdued voices and car doors closing reached Donal on the hill. Behind him, he heard Robert's voice raised in anger. Donal was glad most of the mourners were already getting into their cars. Robert stalked off down the hill toward his car. He still walked with a slight limp from the fight with Jason Strickland when they were teenagers.

Donal glanced over at Johnnie, signaled him to change instrumentals. Johnnie nodded and started playing "Girl from the North Country," one of Donal's favorites.

Donal moved down the hill, intending to talk to Robert. Brid met him at the bottom.

"I failed her," Donal said as he leaned over to hug her. It was meant only for her to hear.

"She is finally at peace, Donal."

"Do you think so?"

"Yes. Take care."

"I am sorry for your loss," Tomás said, as he helped Brid into their car.

Rhyianna hugged Donal. Before getting into the car, she put her hand on his arm. "We won't be coming to the house. It's too much noise for mother."

Donal nodded and watched as they drove off.

"What a beautiful young lady. She reminds me of Rónán at that age."

Donal turned to Robert. "She should. We are cousins several times removed. Please don't upset your brother, not at a time like this."

"What we talked about is nothing that concerns you," Robert said. "Donald was telling me the other day that you are an executive officer under Grandfather."

"That's true."

"That means that I could end up working for you."

"More important, you won't be working for your uncle Billy."

"Damn!"

"You could always get a real job, Rob." Donal regretted saying it, but it was too late to take back the words.

Robert scowled at him. Donal was thankful when Donald joined them.

"Dad, Martin and Rónán are waiting for you."

"Thank you, Donald. I'll see both of you back at the house." Donal started back up the hill, stopped, and turned back to Robert. "Rhyianna isn't your half sister if that is what you are thinking."

Donal turned and continued up the hill. This would be the hardest part.

It would soon be final.

Jenny was never coming back.

At the top, Martin waited for him, holding a bouquet of long-stem Sterling Silver roses, not really silver in color, more of a delicate light purple. There was one rose for each of the years Rónán knew Jennifer.

Donal took the bouquet from Martin and moved over to his son. Rón stood, and together they walked to the coffin and placed the flowers on the top, watching as it was lowered into the ground.

Donal waited.

When his son didn't make a move to leave, he placed his arm around him and said gently, "Time to go."

Rónán said, "No. I can't leave her here. It'll get cold out here tonight." Donal caught him and pulled him back from the edge. Martin moved forward to help.

Now that it was over, Donal had to find a way to keep Rón from going over to the Strickland mansion on Weathervane Lane and confront Jenny's father about his treatment of his daughter.

Together they walked down the hill.

Donal knew who was really to blame for Jenny's death. Yes, her father had a hand in it. But the real blame was his. He forced everything from his mind except helping his son cope.

Chapter Twenty

Clancy parked in the riverside parking lot. He was late. *Damn, I should have left earlier.* He hadn't allowed for the late-morning traffic on Main Street.

He hurried across the parking lot and entered O'Flaherty's by the back door. Neither Thomas nor Tabitha were around.

Down the bar, at the register, Clancy watched one of the servers. The young man ran the credit card though the VeriFone for an approval. Just as Clancy started to turn away, he noticed the young man place the card against a handheld device. The movement was so slight that most people would have missed it.

Clancy shook his head. He would pass the information on to Donal as soon as possible. He hurried up the stairs to number-two snug. The door was open. He was surprised to find Steve Spydell standing just inside the door. Steve was known around town as "Stevey the Spider." He was the mayor's right-hand man.

"Surprised to see you here, Clancy."

"I'm not a member of the merchants group," Clancy said and turned away from Steve. Lily Cheng was addressing the group.

Donal and Martin stood along the wall on the other side of the room.

Seeing Clancy, Donal nodded at him.

Every time Clancy saw Donal at one of these meetings, he got the impression that Donal was an exotic bird among Rock Doves. It was not just his good looks, his height, or athletic build. It was his presence, the way he walked. He looked more like a lord mayor than their present Mayor Pat Junior ever would.

Martin was another matter. He looked tough. When he had played for the Chicago Bears, Clancy had known many linemen on the team who thought they were tough. Martin could probably beat them all, including Clancy.

Clancy pulled himself back to the meeting.

"Why do you care?" shouted the owner of the Wildflower Coffee Shop. "All you and your father have to do is move your restaurant over to the new mall."

There were grumbles of agreement from around the room.

Donal moved to the front and held up his hands to silence the group before things got out of hand. Lily Cheng sat down. The younger males among the merchants were giving her the once-over, wondering what their chances were with her. Lily was watching Donal with an intensity that meant only one thing - she had a thing for him.

"We can't stop the new mall," Donal said, "or the condos they are building out that way. If we stick together, make improvements to Main Street, we can get through this. Keep people coming downtown to shop and eat."

The merchants looked around, nodded at each other. Someone in the back yelled, "You can move to the new mall too, but what about us?"

Steve chuckled, which gave Clancy the impression that he knew what was going to happen here this afternoon.

"You're right," Donal said. "I can move my pub to the new mall. The question is, do I want to? No. I like the location I have right now, and I am willing to fight to keep it where it is."

"We can't afford to update our shops inside, much less the exterior," said the owner of the Emporium.

"Let me see what I can come up with. Let's meet again next week, on Tuesday, same time."

As the group broke up, Donal shook hands with each man and woman gathered and had a word for each of them.

Steve said to Clancy, "Well, I was hoping to address the crowd. I hate to give them bad news. I'll tell Donal, and he can pass on the information to the merchants."

Steve didn't look as though he hated it at all. In fact, he looked as if he was enjoying the thought of giving Donal bad news.

"I don't know why Donal is so upset about the new mall. He wins either way."

"Why don't you ask him?" Clancy said and walked over to join Martin. Steve tagged along behind him.

"Sorry I missed the meeting."

"Not too much new. I can give you the highlights," Martin said.

"I need to speak with Donal," Steve said.

"What about?" Donal asked as he joined them.

"The president of the Prescott Bank stopped by to talk to the mayor today." Steve paused, a satisfied look on his face. "The bank can't help with the loans."

"Steve, it doesn't matter. I can come up with the money through another source."

Steve looked surprised. "So you got your late wife's father to back you."

Clancy waited to see where this was going. There wasn't any love lost between Donal and Steve.

"Where it comes from isn't any of your business."

"I don't understand why you are so concerned about the merchants," Steve said, upset. "I don't see you as someone who would man the barricades, so to speak, or defend anything."

"It is easy for you as the mayor's gilly. You don't have a worry in the world," Donal said. "But for those of us with families to take care of, it is a lot harder."

Clancy had heard the term "gilly" before. In fact, he had looked it up. Donal was using it in the broadest way. He doubted if Steve understood what it meant. From the look on Steve's face, he knew he had been insulted and didn't like it at all.

"I have seen firsthand what happens to a town after a mega-mall opens up," Donal said. "When I first came to the States, I went out west, worked for a small merchant on a Main Street very much like ours here.

"He was a hardworking man. So were his wife and son. The whole town was made up of good, hardworking people. After the mall opened, everyone shopped there instead, ate at the overpriced restaurants.

"My friend was one among many who lost everything, their businesses and their homes. He started to drink, to the point that you knew he would end up living in a bottle." Donal paused. "I won't let that to happen to my friends here."

Steve looked uncomfortable.

"If you will excuse me, I need to get the cleanup going," Donal said as he pulled out his estate-linc and moved away.

◦◦◦

Over a quiet lunch, Clancy sat with Donal and Martin in number-two snug. Donal was relaxed, telling jokes and thoroughly enjoying the moment.

"Funny," Clancy said, "I see you as the opposite of what Steve said."

"Really?" Donal said and laughed. "How do you see me?"

"I see you in the front line, at the barricade, wielding that broadsword of yours. Shouting to your men. Cutting down each Sasanach as they try to assault you."

Silence fell between them.

Martin, who was just lifting his glass to his mouth, stared at him over the rim.

Damn, did I say something wrong. He was relieved when Donal laughed, and so did Martin.

"You have me confused with Cuhulian."

Glad that he hadn't insulted his friend, Clancy decided to change the subject. "Do you use a cloud for your computer system?"

"No. We have our own system," Donal said.

"Then you monitor your own camera system?"

"Yes, we do," Donal said, as he moved his plate away to clear a space. "I can show you. I am sure it is similar to the one you use." He moved his tablet onto the table and turned it on. He opened a folder, and a list of cameras appeared on the screen.

"Are they checked often?"

"They are checked once a week," Martin said.

"Key in the bar camera." Clancy glanced at his watch. "Let's say for about an hour and...ten minutes ago."

"I don't see what you are looking for."

"Try the back camera for about an hour and twenty minutes."

On the screen appeared a picture of Clancy crossing the parking lot.

"Now from that time stamp, check the bar camera," Clancy said.

Donal keyed in the new time stamp.

On the screen, the server Clancy had observed earlier was just entering the bar area. He moved down the bar to the register. The server placed the card against a handheld device. It was so quick that even when the camera images were checked, it would go unnoticed.

"Play it again, in slow motion," Clancy said.

Donal looked closer. "Damnation!" He keyed the program to run again and turned the screen so Martin could see what was going on.

"What the?" Martin said. "Did I just see him swipe a credit card a second time? We hardly ever have trouble like that. He picked the wrong restaurant to do it at. Should I call Thomas up here?"

"We'll talk to him later. Thanks for the information, Clancy," Donal said as he stood and walked over the refrigerator and took two Harps and a Sam Adams out.

"After you warn Thomas, you might check with the sheriff and see if other places have had similar problems. Sometimes thieves like him move from restaurant to restaurant."

"I'll give him a call," Donal said. "Thanks."

"I have more info that might be good or bad, depending on how you look at it," Clancy said.

"What kind of information?"

"Strickland's chauffeur, Jeff Denton, has always come into Stan's from time to time. Since Jenny's funeral, he comes in two or three times a week. Always parks in the back, so anyone passing on the Old Chicago Road wouldn't see the car."

"Do you think he knows something about what happened to Jenny that day?" Donal asked.

"Don't know. But he was driving that day," Clancy said. "He keeps to himself. Doesn't really talk to any of the waitresses."

"Interesting. How long does he stay?" Donal said, sitting back.

"He stays about an hour." Clancy smiled. "Long enough for someone to come over and talk to him."

"Thanks for the heads-up, Clancy. Call me next time he comes in."

After Clancy left, Donal went downstairs to talk to Thomas. Music playing in the side room drew him there. He stood among several customers listening to Johnnie Coffey play his fiddle while Siobhán Dunn sang.

Martin came to stand beside Donal. "She has a voice as beautiful as her face."

"Yes, she does. I think we should invite her to dinner on Sunday."

"Looking for someone for Rónán or one of the twins?"

Donal wasn't really thinking about his sons. He was thinking about Martin. He was overdue to get married.

"I'm going to let the sheriff handle our new problem," Donal said in Irish.

One of the customers moved closer to Donal. "Is the side room open?"

Donal motioned to Johnnie, and he nodded.

"Yes, it is."

CHAPTER
TWENTY-ONE

After dinner three nights later, up in their third-floor apartment, Donal sat relaxing with Moya over drinks. Moya refused a drink and asked for tea. This was their favorite time of day, when it was just the two of them.

"I would love to have an herb garden," Moya said.

"There is a nice area that gets plenty of sun down near the garage." Donal was pleased that Moya was going to get out more. He hoped it wouldn't change now that Jenny was gone. "Fionn can help you with the layout. Just let me know what you need, and I'll order it."

Moya smiled at Donal. "My foster father and your son would be amazed at how well you live here."

"I am sure they would be."

"Fionn is undecided in how he can serve you," Moya said. "Has he spoken to you?"

"No," Donal said. "I know he was considering becoming a holy man."

"Has there ever been a holy man with the Power?"

"Yes" Donal said. "The abbot I studied under, I am sure, had the Power. He wore a gold ring just like I do. I'll speak with Fionn."

"If we are blessed by the Father with children. I was wondering..." Moya stopped.

Donal knew what worried her. Who would inherit the house, the land, and who would take over if something happened to him? Until this moment, he hadn't given it too much thought. He had many years ahead of him. If they had a child, it was something he would have to address.

"Are you...?"

The knock on the door stopped what he was going to ask Moya.

"Come in," Donal called.

Martin stepped into the room.

"Is there a problem?" Donal asked.

"I hate to bother you, but Clancy called."

Donal sat up. He had no choice. He needed to talk to Jeff Denton. "Moya, I hate to end this so soon, but I need to go into town."

Moya looked from Donal to Martin. She didn't say anything, just nodded.

Martin drove the Land Rover.

On the dashboard, Donal had placed a high-tech jamming device before they left Forest Lake. As they entered Stan's parking lot, he turned it on. It would blank out the cameras in the back and make it impossible to make a call from the back parking lot. Martin parked the Land Rover at the back, near the end, well away from the chauffeur's car.

Martin got out, and with a low-tech device, a pin, he let the air out of the front tire on the driver's side of Denton's car so it wouldn't be missed. He got back into the Land Rover.

Now they waited.

Less then half an hour later, Jeff Denton came out the back door and headed toward his car. He stopped halfway from his car, before he hurried forward to examine the tire.

"Damn," he yelled as he pulled out his cell phone, keyed in a number, and swore again. "What the hell is going on?"

Donal said, "Time for us to rescue him before he goes back inside."

"Problem?" Donal asked.

"Yes, I..." Jeff stopped, then shouted, "You! You did this to my car?"

"Did what?" Donal asked, guileless.

"Wrecked my tire, that's what."

"We were just going inside for a drink, thought we could help you."

"Help me! Damn."

"Listen, Mr. Denton, I can fix it for you," Martin offered.

"Yeah. And what do I have to do for this help?"

"Nothing," Donal said. "But you could tell me what happened at the post office between Strickland and his daughter, and later at the house on Weathervane Lane."

"This is a set up," Jeff said as he headed back toward the roadhouse.

"Eíst, listen," Donal said as he caught the chauffeur by the wrist. He put his thumb on the palm of Denton's hand, and the other fingers on the back. "Just relax."

Jeff relaxed as asked. A spaced-out expression replaced his angry look.

"Now I want you to walk over to my car with me while Martin fixes your tire. Sit in the passenger seat, and we can have a friendly talk."

Donal nodded to Martin, then turned and followed Jeff over to the Land Rover. Once inside, he didn't waste time.

"What happened at the post office?"

"We were driving down Main Street, when her father spotted Jenny crossing over to go to the post office on Elm. Strickland had me circle around and park on Elm, not in the parking lot. We waited. When she came out, I got out and called to her."

Donal took Jeff by the hand again.

Immediately, Donal was there on Elm Street, with Jeff calling to Jenny. She hesitated, unsure of what to do.

"Miss Jenny, your mother would like a word with you," Jeff Denton said, opening the car door for her.

Jenny still hesitated, but it was too late. He pushed her into the car and closed the door behind her. He jumped into the driver's seat and hit the button to lock the doors.

The limo pulled up in front of the Strickland mansion on Weathervane Lane.

"Should I wait to take Miss Jenny back into town?" Jeff asked.

"Yes, yes," Strickland said, not really listening to his chauffeur.

Strickland pulled a struggling Jenny into the house, down the hall, and into the study. The door closed with a bang. Out in the living room, Jeff heard Strickland shouting at his daughter.

Jenny shouted back.

Silence followed.

The silence was scarier than the shouting. What was going on now? The housekeeper brought a teacart and knocked on the study door. Strickland called for her to enter.

In that brief moment, while the door was open, Jeff saw Strickland sitting on the couch with his arm around Jenny. The door closed. That was the last time he saw her alive.

When the housekeeper left, Strickland came to the door.

"Jeff, you can go off duty. Jenny is going to stay for the night."

"It was later, when the housekeeper discovered that Jenny wasn't in her room, that they searched the house and found the attic door open on the third floor."

Donal broke the contact with Jeff at the stairs leading up to the attic. He didn't want to see Jenny hanging from the rafters, didn't want that image imprinted on his memory.

"I found her in the attic. Dear God, what have I had a hand in?"

"Relax," Donal told Jeff. "Just lean back and relax."

First it was a blinding light, then a sharp rap on the window with something hard. "What the hell is going on in there?"

Donal put his right hand up to shield his eyes from the light. "Turn that off, or face it away from me."

The light was turned down toward the ground. "Step out of the car. Now! Keep your hands where I can see them."

Donal did as asked. "Who are you?"

"FBI. Turn around and assume the position."

Donal seemed to have stepped into a cop drama.

"I want to see some ID first."

The man fumbled in his pocket and produced a thin folder. He flipped it open and held it out for Donal to see.

"It's too dark here," Donal said, taking the folder.

"Don't try anything stupid." The man turned the flashlight so the light fell onto the folder. He glanced into the car. "What is wrong with him?"

"Just taking a rest," Donal said.

In his mind, he heard Rón's words, *"I had the feeling last week I was followed into town."*

"Here. Everything looks in order," Donal said and held the folder out toward the special agent. At the last second, he let it slip from his fingers. "Sorry."

The agent tried to catch the folder and lost his balance.

Donal moved forward. "Let me help you." He placed his thumb on his palm and the rest of his fingers on the back of the agent's hand. The agent fought him, or rather, tried to fight him. It was over in seconds. "Martin?"

"Here," Martin said as he stepped from the shadows at the edge of the parking lot.

"I didn't hear him. When I did, it was too late to do anything to help you."

"FBI, one of Roger's friends I would say. I was wrong. They aren't after Michael Lafferty. They are after me. The question is, why?"

∞

Donal stopped to talk to Martin at the foot of the stairs to the third floor.

"I don't know whether I should be upset or amused by the FBI looking into Tolan, O'Brien, and Scanlon Enterprise. Strange, I stay out of politics." Donal shook his head.

"That is true," Martin said. "But think of all your employees that hold American citizenship. They are politically active even if you aren't."

"Funny, I doubt that Johnnie Coffey will ever understand what he started when he came here looking for me."

"I wonder how many more of our people are out there." Martin glanced up the stairs. "How many more will show up. Donal..."

Moya was leaning over the newel post on the landing, watching them. She looked both relieved and upset at the same time.

"Moya, has something happened?" Donal said, as he hurried up the stairs.

As he rounded the newel post, Moya fell into his arms. He held her against his chest.

"Darling, did something happen?"

Moya shook her head.

Donal lifted her head and kissed her.

"What happened, mo ghrá?" Her tears tasted salty on his lips.

"I saw the look in Martin's eyes. It is a look I am familiar with. I have seen it many times when my foster father, Lord Rónán, rode out to deal with problems. I worried about you. I am so pleased that you are back safe."

"Oh, Moya. I didn't want to worry you, but I see I did anyway," he said, and brushed her hair back. As soon as he released her, she hugged him again.

"What if you did not come back? You would never know I am with child," she murmured against his chest.

"What?" That is why she was worried about the position of her children here at Forest Lake.

When she looked up at him and nodded, Donal kissed her again. He was beyond happy. It was what they both wanted.

"Have you thought about names yet?" Donal asked.

"If it is a boy, Tuathall or Rogan. If the baby is a girl, either Mór, Fionnuala, or your mother's name."

"We will call her after your mother."

From the landing, Martin cleared his throat loud enough for the couple to hear. "Excuse me, is everything all right?"

Donal had forgotten that Martin was with him. He was standing on the landing. He didn't ask what was going on. He waited. His eyes said that he would help in any way possible.

"Everything is under control."

"So this is where everyone is," Rónán said from below. "Sally Brown wants everyone to try her latest cake, see if it is good enough to send to the bake sale at St. Anthony's.

"Tell her we will be right down," Donal said. "Plus we have good news for everyone.

After seeing that Moya was comfortable in bed, Donal made the rounds around the property, a job Martin usually did. Still not sleepy, he entered the chapel and closed the door behind him. When the light didn't come on, he placed his right palm on the wall to the right of the door, and a rectangular panel lit up. He keyed in the program for sunrise.

At the front of the chapel, behind the altar, the stained-glass window came to life, as if it were really on an outside wall facing east at daybreak.

"Awesome." Rónán's voice came from the far end of the last pew.

"Would you like some company?"

"Sure, Da."

Donal moved over and sat down sideways.

"This is such a beautiful room, yet I see nothing of you in it."

"This is your mother's idea of what a chapel should look like. More of an Italian feel than Celtic. I am used to much more austere chapels." Donal paused, before he said, "I hope you weren't upset by our good news tonight?"

"Growing up here, I had my brothers, Martin and Carl, to play with. Now Caitlín will have someone to play with and probably boss around." Rónán frowned. "Robert called while you were out this evening."

"I hope he didn't upset you again?"

"I barely know the twins anymore. Especially Robert," Rónán said. "He wants me to finish my degree out east. Stay with either Donald or him."

"A change might do you some good."

"Yes, I know." Rónán paused. "Do you believe there is a heaven?"

"Yes."

"I was talking to Mánus when he was here. I asked him about the Road of Life and Death. He said I should talk to you about it."

Donal hesitated. It was a complicated subject that he would rather not get into. Instead he said, "What do you want to know, son?"

"What is it like?"

"To me, I see a long road through a wasteland, no, more like a wilderness. The road goes on and on. There is a bright light at the end."

Rónán turned to face his father. "What is at the end? Heaven, hell, nothingness?"

"I have never been to the end. I think that when I reach it, I won't be able to come back and tell anyone what heaven is like."

"So you think it is heaven?"

"Yes."

"You have come back from the road?"

"Yes." Donal paused. "Like many people who have experienced things like that, it wasn't my time."

Sometimes, you need to be reminded that it isn't your time to die so you don't just let go.

"Perhaps the Father sent me back for a reason. It allows me to help others whose time isn't right to pass on." Donal waited a minute before he decided to change the subject. "Perhaps a trip out east would be good for you."

"Yes, a change would be good for me, but where? Surely not to Robert's idea of life, two-hour lunches and cut out of work early. Besides, I will need to get back to my classes soon, so nothing that would take too much time," Rónán said. "And there is my little girl to think of."

Anywhere but here.

"Perhaps Cwillan."

"What?"

"You heard me. You are going back to get Dobailein. I would love to join you."

"And just leave Caitlín with Moya?"

"I am sure I can work things out with Moya and the Ladies."

Rón had already made up his mind.

CHAPTER
TWENTY-TWO

Early autumn fog hung over the valley, making the stables and studio building look unfamiliar, even strange, in the early morning light. Alvin hurried from the studio building where he had his room.

His plan was to cut through the first stable. He wanted to smoke a cigerette behind the second stable before reporting to Carl. He thought it was dumb not to allow smoking in his room or around the stables.

He stopped.

Someone was standing at the fence, stroking Cinnamon. The fog made it hard to see clearly. Cold sweat broke out on his forehead.

Jenny.

Jenny had come back to haunt him, come back because of the tea he'd given her.

"How are you, Cinnamon?"

Alvin relaxed.

It was Moya. Perhaps he should offer her some tea. Before he could, Martin appeared out of the fog to stand beisde her.

"Morning, Moya," Martin said. "The Ladies said they saw you heading down here."

"I worry about Cinnamon. We both miss Jenny so much."

Alvin moved to the corner of the building, where he could watch them and not be seen. He wished they were talking in English, not Old Irish. He understood a little modern Irish, but could make no sense of the old version Moya and Martin were speaking.

He wished he was on better terms with Martin. He could offer both of them some of his speical tea. But he had a plan to fix that problem.

Martin and Moya turned and disappeared into the fog, in the direction of the stairs to the house.

Alvin cut through the first stable. There was still time for a smoke.

CHAPTER TWENTY-THREE

Donal shook off the memories of his past and headed back to their camp at Lough Airgead.

In the morning, he walked up to Silver Falls with Rónán. He stood with one foot placed on the huge flat boulder that formed a platform that hung over the canyon, toward the falls. Water rushed by beyond Rónán. He was ready to pull his son back from the edge if he got any crazy ideas in his head.

As they rode up to Lough Airgead, Donal had noticed how dry everything was. Even the water coming over the edge was a mere trickle of what usually rushed on to the lake.

Rónán turned and smiled at him. "You can relax. I am not going to do anything stupid." He looked around. "I can see why you like coming back here. It's such a beautiful place."

"It is a hard and very dangerous life here. You grow up fast if you want to survive."

"I know, you're right. But in ways more peaceful than home, in ways more civilized." Rónán looked around. "Is there a way to get to the top?"

"Yes, there are some old stone steps back down the trail that go to the top. Legend says that a witch lives up there."

"You never went up to see?" Rónán asked.

"No." Donal smiled and shook his head. "Strange that they believe in witches here. Ireland didn't have the terrible witch hunts that occurred on mainland Europe. At least, not among the native Irish people. I don't think Déaglán brought the belief with him."

"If you had to come back here," Rónán asked, "what would you miss from your other home?"

"That's easy," Donal said. He smiled at the surprise in Rónán's eyes. His son had expected him to say ice cream, modern whiskey, or central heating. "I would miss you."

Thrown for a second at his father's answer, Rón didn't answer him right away. "Perhaps I would come with you."

"You have always been the closest, Rón, but...I would never ask *you* to make that big of a sacrifice. Martin would come back with me, Fionn too. Moya would go wherever I go. But you Rón or one of the twins? No."

"Do you think Robert or Donald will ever come home?"

"You're asking me? Son, you're the one going to school, and who likes to joke about calling yourself a head doctor. Donald has already made overtures to come home, but he has to make the decision. I didn't throw him out, it is his move. Robert is another matter."

"Robert lives in a bottle," Rón said. "I don't know if he will ever change. But my faith more than my profession tells me someday, something will force him to make a stand."

"I hope you're right, Rón."

CHAPTER
TWENTY-FOUR

The next morning they had a visitor. Donal and Rónán were just returning with their morning catch. The stranger was talking with Vél. As they approached, the man stopped to acknowledge them.

The stranger offered his name, Lun Dubh, without being asked. His golden tan spoke of time spent further south. There was no way for Donal to know if he was one of Feargus's men.

Donal invited him to break bread with them.

As they ate, Donal asked, "What brings you up here this late in the season?"

"I was born not far from here, the small village between here and the Judgment Tree. This is a peaceful place. I thought I would see if there was snow on the peaks."

It was a strange answer. He could see if there was snow on the peaks from the valley floor. Why come up here?

"Have you been here long?" Lun Dubh asked.

Now we get down to why he is really here.

"We have been here six mornings. You are the first person we have seen." Lun Dubh looked disappointed. Donal waited for a comment. When he didn't get one, he said, "There were riders up here a half-moon past, sometime after Lunasa."

"Many?"

"Several mounted and unmounted horses. They took the South Airgead Pass, going to either Moll-Dur or Solaria."

"I see," is all Lun Dubh said.

As soon as the meal was over, Lun Dubh thanked them for their kindness and said, "May the Father and Son watch over you." He mounted his horse and rode back toward the plains.

"I wonder who this stranger is?" Vél asked.

"Beon," Donal said to the boy, "go as far as the path down to the plains. See where this man is going. Be careful."

Beon ran back up the path to the point where it started to turn downward before it joined a trail to the Great Plains. He kept close to the trees.

❧

Lun Dubh, sitting up in a tall tree, waited. His horse was hidden well back in the trees. He was disappointed when he saw the boy coming along the path.

The boy passed beneath him, unaware that Lun Dubh watched him.

Too bad. Lun Dubh had hoped that the tall light-haired man would follow him.

After the boy hurried back up the path, he climbed down from the tree and walked to where his horse was tethered. He needed to hurry so he could report to his lord.

❦

An owl on the hunt, only a dark shadow as it passed over Lough Airgead, just discernible to the human eye, flew north. Donal watched the bird of prey until he lost sight of it in the darkness. He pulled his cloak tighter around him, kept the hood up not only for warmth, but because it covered his hair and cast a shadow over his face.

Vél would relieve him soon.

The nights up here were cold. Donal shivered. Lun Dubh's disappearance had unnerved him. It was better to lose a little sleep standing guard than to lose your life.

The curlew call came minutes later. Donal answered with an up trill, then down again, and stepped from the shadows.

"This is like old times," Vél said as he came up the path.

"We were younger men then."

"You gave your cloak to my mother to keep my younger sisters warm. I knew even before that night on the Dubh River that you were the right man to follow."

CHAPTER TWENTY-FIVE

Their time at Lough Airgead was growing short. Donal and Rónán made one last trip up to the falls. In the morning, they would ride to the crossroads to meet Ciarán and Dobailein. The wind had shifted, the air was cool and misty, and the flat boulder shiny and slippery with spray. Father and son stood at the edge of the trees and talked.

At the sound of a cry for help, Donal turned.

Vél's son ran up the trail. He didn't wait to try to catch his breath. "My father," he gasped, "has need of you. There are men stealing our horses."

Donal turned to Rónán. "Stay with Beon. I'll go see what is going on below." He turned and hurried down the trail. Without their horses, it would take them more time than they had to get to the western crossroads.

Behind him, he heard Rón calling to him to wait. His son was right. Two men would be better than one. Donal didn't slow to let him catch up. He hurried on.

He had to be careful. It would be easy to trip on an exposed tree root or get caught by an overhanging branch on the narrow, overgrown path.

He hurried anyway.

Horse thieves meant trouble. He glanced back. The trail behind him was empty. Then a second later, further back, his son came into view, trying to catch up.

Donal cleared the trees and turned onto the main trail. Vél was lying on the ground. The small fenced-in area where they kept their horses stood empty. Donal knelt to see to his old friend. He was thankful to find Vél not badly hurt. He would suffer only a headache from a blow to the head.

From the beach below came the whinny of horses.

Rónán knelt down beside him.

"See to Vél," Donal said.

Donal hurried back through the trees and ran down the path to the beach. If he hurried, he might be in time to stop the thieves. The horses were well beyond him as he made the bottom of the path.

Hearing a shout of "Behind you!" from above, he turned to see a lone horseman bearing down on him, trying to run him down. At the last second, Donal dodged to the right. Years ago he had learned it was impossible to stop a running horse.

He pulled out his dagger and threw it so the hilt would strike the rider. It hit him square in the back of the head. Screaming, the rider yanked on the reins to turn his small horse, causing the animal to almost sit down in the loose sand as it struggled to regain its balance.

Donal ran to the rider, caught him, and dragged him backward onto the sand.

The fight didn't last long. Half stunned from being hit by the dagger, a couple of blows to the chin and the rider was out cold.

Donal picked up his dagger and ran to the horse and cut the girth. After pulling the saddle away, he mounted the small, wiry horse and rode it in the old Irish way, with only a blanket beneath him. He urged the horse forward in pursuit of the thieves.

∽

Feargus, High King of Cwillan, led Tinreach, his stallion, along the ridge, trying to hurry. He was well aware of the chance he took. His stallion could stumble and break a leg. He was surprised when he learned that his father was up here. Perhaps it was not too late to save Cullan Donal from his own selfless acts. Behind him, Lonán, Apprentice to his Guardian, tried to keep up. Feargus called to the men and boys in his party to hurry.

Once he reached the beach, Feargus stopped only long enough to see his father riding the small horse in the strangest fashion. He leaned all the way forward and had his legs pulled well up on the small horse. It was said that Cullan Donal could ride any horse. At this moment, Feargus did not doubt that his father could even ride a púca.

Another man, a stranger, ran down the path behind his men. Startled, Feargus turned to stare at him. He was looking into the light eyes of his father. This must be his youngest brother, Rónán, whom he had never met. Feargus had an unfamiliar feeling at the sight. Strange, was he jealous of this man? He did not have time to puzzle out why.

The young man stared back at him, as startled as he was. Feargus acknowledged him by nodding, turned to his horse and mounted. He called to Seta and Colm to look after the thief, and the others to follow him.

How stupid he must have looked to the High King, just standing their staring at him, his mouth open.

"That is the High King," Rónán said more to himself than to the young men tying up the thief.

"Where do you come from that you do not know Feargus, lord of Cwillan and lord of the children of Déaglán?" the older of the two men asked.

Rónán didn't answer him.

He stood in awe watching his father, who had caught up with the horses and managed to turn a dozen or more and head them toward the water, then around and back down the beach. The horse thieves didn't challenge him. They rode on with what was left of their stolen horses. Feargus and his men were helping round up the animals.

CHAPTER TWENTY-SIX

In private, Donal made the introductions.

Both Feargus and Rónán seemed wary of each other. Feargus smiled, stepped forward and embraced his younger brother. "In my heart, I am pleased to meet you."

Rónán mumbled that he was please to meet him also. For a second he forgot and started to speak in English. He caught himself and repeated his words in Irish.

Feargus turned to Donal. "We need to talk."

"Will you be okay, Da?" Rónán asked in English.

"Of course."

Vél joined Rónán on the beach. Seeing the young man's discomfort, the older man tried to reassure him by saying, "Do not worry about your father. No harm will come to him from his eldest son."

"You know they are father and son?"

"Yes. I was with your father when Artúr tried to drive us across the Dubh River, and again at Carracán. Cullan

Donal is an ageless warrior. There is no reason to worry about him."

Rónán wasn't reassured at all.

Feargus seemed too much like his brother Robert. The only physical differences between the half brothers was that Feargus's hair was darker, his stature more like Donal's. He wore a well-trimmed beard and mustache, and pulled his shoulder-length hair back at the neck, held in place by a leather thong with ornate gold tips.

If something happens to Donal, it will be on my head, Rónán thought. He had caused the problem that forced his father to bring him to Cwillan, and why they were here at Silver Lake.

"What did you do for my father?" Rónán asked.

"How does an army travel?"

That was easy. "By horse or by foot."

"No, an army travels on its stomach. With the help of another man, Rogan, I saw that we had supplies for man and beast."

CHAPTER TWENTY-SEVEN

Donal and Feargus walked along the beach to the inlet. From there they walked up to the lower falls. His son moved up to the edge of the large pool formed by rushing water from above.

He turned to Donal. "What does "Da" mean?"

"It is short for 'father' in my new language," Donal said. What was his son doing up here so late in the year? With only a dozen warriors and the unproven Youths with him? Before he could ask, Feargus spoke.

"Marriage suits you." Feargus smiled. "How is Moya? Is she with child yet?"

"Moya is doing well. She is with child. It will be a winter birth."

"Winter is a good time for a son. Children are a comfort in our old age." Feargus studied him. "I was surprised when I received word that you were up here. Ciarán is waiting for you at the western crossroad."

So Lun Dubh was one of his men. Then all the things that had led up to his bringing Rónán to Cwillan filled his thoughts: his son's marriage, his grand-daughter, and a young life cut off all too short.

Donal cleared his mind. "Rónán lost his wife. He was in need of a change."

"I am sorry to hear this sad news. Was she sick long?" Feargus asked.

Donal moved closer to the edge of the pool. He picked up a flat stone and skipped it across the water. It hit four times before disappearing beneath the dark water.

He turned back to Feargus. "Not sick. She took her own life."

Taking your life was against everything they believed in. Life was a gift from the Father. To throw it away was a terrible thing, a sin. He expected Feargus to comment on this fact.

To his surprise, Feargus said, "I am sorry that my brother has lost someone he loved, that you have lost a daughter of your heart."

"It is a terrible loss," Donal said. "His daughter will grow up without a mother."

"I would think at his age he could yet have many children," Feargus said.

Changing the subject, Donal asked, "How bad is it?"

"How bad?" Feargus said.

"My heart is glad to see you," Donal paused. How could he say this with diplomacy? "But it is late in the year. You should be back at the Fortress of Cwillan seeing that everything is in order for the coming winter."

Feargus stiffened at Donal's words. "My reachtaire takes care of supplies."

"I have seen how good you are with numbers. You could do it yourself in half the time. So I wonder why you are out with the Youths so close to Samhain?"

Feargus didn't comment.

Donal figured the Youths were a cover for him to go from holding to holding. But why, was the real question.

"It is good to see you, Father," Feargus said. He moved past Donal. The conversation was over. "There is nothing wrong."

Before they reached the encampment the warriors and the Youths were setting up not far from where Vél had pitched their tents, Donal asked his son, "Do you plan to follow the horse thieves? Once beyond the narrow pass, it is a two or three mornings ride to Moll-Dur or Solaria."

"I think not," Feargus said. "I will send one of the Youths to the western crossroad and have Ciarán meet you up here. You will stay until we try the thief?"

Donal told his son he would give witness at the trial, and thanked him for having Ciarán join him here. That way the few days he had left here could be spent with his two sons.

"I would like Vél to rest for a morning or two. I could use the service of one of the Youths."

"Speak with Lonán."

Lonán accompanied Donal to where the Youths were setting up their tents. Seeing the second-in-command's Apprentice approaching, they came to attention.

"The kin of our lord, Feargus, has need of the service of one of the Youths while he is with us."

Ruadrí, the leader of the Youths stepped forward. "Will I send one to you, or would you rather choose yourself?"

Donal looked over the Youths. In the back stood two older boys, well past their middle summers. When he glanced at them, they lowered their heads. Passed over many times, they did not think they would be picked for this duty either. Due to their age, this would be their last season with the Youths.

"What of those two at the back?"

"Yes, lord. Which one?" the leader asked.

"The taller of the two." As soon as he said this, Donal noticed the taller one looked at his companion, who nodded as if to say go, donot worry about me. "I would like the other one also."

Ruadrí begin to protest. Lonán cut him off. "It is decided. Seta, Colm, step forward. You will go with your lord's kin. You are excused from practice, unless you are given leave."

Donal set Seta and Colm to arrange a large cook fire for both Donal's small party and Feargus's men.

CHAPTER
TWENTY-EIGHT

The next day, after practicing their fighting skills, Feargus's men and the Youths gathered on the beach. A rough pitch, with goals at each end, was marked off in the sand, close to the water, where the sand was firmer. The Youths, including Seta and Colm, and enough of Feargus's men to make up teams, started a stick-and-ball game. It took a few minutes before Rónán realized that they were hurling.

"This reminds me of that trip we took a long time ago. I was pretty little, so all I remember is one of the players on the Chicago team gave Martin a carmán, his stick, after the game," Rónán said.

"Those were good times, going to watch our Chicago team play Indianapolis."

They were all good times before Robert had the fight with Jason Strickland and he began to change.

"I've seen Martin's stick. It is old."

"Very old, passed down through his family. He is a good player, but he was never interested in playing with the Chicago team."

"Are you a hurler, Da?"

"I haven't played in years," Donal said, smiling at his son. "I was fair at it, back at that time."

Donal was probably very good at hurling.

Feargus, Lonán, and the men not playing moved over to where Donal and Rónán were standing to watch the game.

"Which team do you favor, Feargus?" Donal asked.

"I like the team Ruadrí is on, he will captain them to victory."

"Then I will favor Seta's team."

"You place much confidence on the brothers, Seta and Colm," Feargus said.

"I do."

Rónán watched the fast-paced game. He wasn't sure he understood all the rules. Over the years the rules, number of players on each team, and the goalposts had changed. Ruadrí's team was good, but Seta, working with his brother and teammates, was better.

Seta's team won.

It was a point system that Rónán didn't understand either. After the game came a lot of good-natured name-calling aimed at the losers.

"Perhaps you are right," Feargus said.

Feargus went down to congratulate the winners and console the losers. After their king left, all the players stripped down and jumped into the lake for a swim. They had to wade out six or seven feet to find deep water.

"What did Feargus mean, Da?"

"I am hoping that he will sponsor the brothers. They both have the qualifications to become loyal men in his personal guard."

As they watched the men and Youths swimming, Rónán glanced down the beach, two men were coming their way along the dune. From their clothing, he made them out to be warriors, even though they weren't in full battle dress. More of Feargus's men, he was sure.

When the warriors were close, the older of the men came down the sand dune and said, "Did your team win?"

Rónán was delighted to see it was Ciarán, one of the Four Horsemen who rode with his father. The years had been kind to him.

Hearing Ciarán's voice, Donal turned with a broad smile on his face and said, "Ciarán," as he embraced his former Guardian.

"I was worried when you did not meet us at the crossroads."

"We came up here, and would have met you, but we ran into Feargus. Now we are together."

"I see you have one of your other sons with you," Ciarán said. He turned and called to the young man to join them.

"Rónán," Ciarán said, "my son, Dobailein. You have met my oldest, Lonán."

Dobailein nodded at him.

So this is Dobailein, the young man who is going to join our household. Rónán found him friendly enough, though something in the young man's eyes gave the impression that leaving Cwillan was not his choice.

Rónán hoped he would fit in at Forest Lake.

CHAPTER TWENTY-NINE

When Rónán woke, he found his father's sleeping place empty. He dressed in a hurry. He was cold again and wanted to put his cloak over his tunic, but knew no one else would. He slipped a jerkin on before leaving the tent.

He found their camp deserted, except for Beon, who sat tending the fire.

"Have you seen my father and the rest of the men?"

"Our lord went for a swim. Your father is with him."

Rónán turned and ran down to the beach.

Feargus's warriors, Lonán, Dobailein, and the Youths, stood to one side. Vél and the brothers, Seta and Colm, stood closer to the water's edge. Everyone was watching the water.

Out in the silvery-green lake, Rónán made out three heads, one of them lighter than the other two. He shuddered to think of swimming in that icy water on a cold morning. Goose bumps rose on his arms, just thinking about it.

Feargus and his father were swimming toward the shore. Farther back, Ciarán brought up the rear. All of a sudden, his father's head disappeared beneath the water. Rónán stepped closer, held his breath, and waited. He let it out with relief when his father's head appeared again.

It was a myth that a person drowning always waved their arms and called for help. Often they sank beneath the water without a sound. Though Vél lived near a desert, he seemed to know this too. He waded out into the water.

Feargus reached the beach first. He stepped from the water, wearing the briefest of underclothes. To Rónán, he looked like a selkie stepping from the sea, his long dark hair plastered to his head, his wet, athletic body shining in the morning light.

Before taking the cloth offered by the leader of the Youths, Feargus slicked the water from his hair with his fingers. He glanced down at Vél.

"It is best to roll up your leggings before entering the water."

Vél did not comment.

The leader of the Youths said, "He thought the old one was in trouble."

Feargus pushed the cloth back at Ruadrí and turned and hurried back into the water. He met Donal as he reached shallow water. Feargus placed his arm around him, and together they walked onto the beach.

Seeing them together, they looked like the king of the selkies and Aodh Ruadh O'Domhnaill returned to reclaim his place in life. Donal turned his head and said something to Feargus meant only for his ears.

Feargus took the cloth from the Ruadrí, flipped it over his shoulder, and started up the trail to their camp.

"You okay?" Rónán asked Donal as they followed Feargus and his men up the beach.

"I'm fine, nothing like an early morning swim to clear your head."

"We were worried when you disappeared beneath the water," Vél said.

"Nothing to worry about."

"Coming out of the water, you looked like Aodh Ruadh O'Domhnaill himself," Rónán said.

"Red Hugh O'Donnell, huh?" Donal smiled, turned, and started up the path.

Realizing what he had said, Rónán hurried to catch up.

"Wait," he called to his father.

Donal stopped at the top.

"I meant your hair color and looks. They say he was the most beautiful man in all of Ireland."

"Keen of eye, red haired, beautiful to behold, smarter than any living man. Not me at all, except for the hair. Though my hair isn't a true red."

"Da, I wasn't drawing a comparison of Red Hugh to you leaving Cwillan." He hurried on to say, "Before we left, Johnnie Coffey was telling me that we come from Ulster. I always thought we were from Munster."

"That is what Johnnie tells me too," Donal said. "I took no offense, Rón."

Rónán watched his father head back to their tent. Now, after all these years, he had let his hero, his father, down. Everything that happened had been his fault. Everything.

"Jenny," he whispered, "why didn't I tell him?"

Ciarán came up the trail. "Come, do not look so sad."

Rónán was astounded. Ciarán had spoken to him in English. He had a thick accent, but it was English.

CHAPTER THIRTY

Baldor, lord of Solaria, stared at the older man. "Surely you joke?"

"No, I am serious. Together we could take the horsemen. Their land is rich."

"Kyfer, my grandfather had an agreement with Cormac's grandfather, the first king of the horsemen. We have renewed that agreement with each new king. I cannot go against Lord Feargus."

"He only has a small band of warriors with him, and two light-haired men, one young, one older."

At mention of the light-haired men, the young man, named Dearg, sitting next to Baldor shifted his position, suddenly interested in the conversation.

"What have you taken from Feargus that he wants back?" Baldor asked.

"I stole one of his stallions and several of his mares. I would have had more, but the older light-haired man interfered. Feargus holds my son."

"The horsemen love to fight. Do not go against them, or you will find your life short, my friend."

"He will have even less men. He will have to send one man to each of the holdings to get help."

Baldor shook his head. "He will send one man to the closest fortress and expect the lord there to send out riders. Give up this folly."

"I will think on it," Kyfer replied, clearly unhappy.

When they were alone, Baldor turned to the young man at his side. "Do you know either of these men, Dearg?"

"Yes. The older one, his name is Cullan."

"I also know him. He is of the direct line of Déaglán, as is Feargus. It is said that the king of Wyneth and Cwillan are kin, by marriage in Cormac's grandfather's time."

"You know a lot about my people," the young man said. "Have you met him?"

"Yes, many summers back."

"The truth is, Déaglán is only a myth. He never existed, nor Brian Mór."

"You are wrong," Baldor said. "It was one of my ancestors that witnessed them come out of the Great Desert. Déaglán brought with him, his wife, children, servants, and a band of warriors. He also brought the beautiful horses with him. Those that survived the desert were the hardiest of his people."

"They are only stories, myths, to tell your children before they go to sleep. I think I will go with Kyfer and see what is going on in my homeland."

"I speak the truth. It is written in one of our old books." Baldor was angry that his friend doubted him. He bit back the harsh words on the tip of his tongue and said, "May the gods watch over you, my friend."

CHAPTER
THIRTY-ONE

The thief's trial was held on the beach. Near the path, two of Feargus's men held the thief with his hands tied behind his back. The other warriors and the Youths stood in two rows facing forward. Feargus stood with his back to the lake, presiding over the trial, with Ciarán and Lonán on each side.

Donal stood to the side with Rónán, Vél, and his son.

Feargus's stance said that this was a serious matter. Due to the absence of his cheif brehon, Tole, Ciarán, who knew the law, would question each witness. The thief was brought forward to stand before Feargus and Ciarán.

"Bring the first witness," Ciarán said.

Vél stepped forward and gave his name.

"Is this one of the men who you caught stealing your horses?"

Vél looked the thief over. "No, lord, I know not this man."

Donal stepped forward next, gave his name as Cullan Donal MacCormac. Adding his father's name as his surname, instead of Tolan. "This man tried to run me down after his companions stole our horses."

"What say you?" Ciarán asked, turning to the accused thief.

"My horse stumbled in the loose sand. I had no intention of riding him down. He misunderstood my actions." He looked around at the assembled men. "I was trying to catch the horse thieves."

Rónán was called forward last.

"Your name?"

"Rónán MacCormac," he said. "From the bluff, I witnessed this man try to ride down my father."

"What do you say in your defense?" Feargus asked the thief.

"He is wrong. He lies. So does the other one."

"Are you saying that my kin lies?" Feargus asked.

The thief looked from Feargus to Donal, but did not answer. Seeing his future, he sank down on his knees in the sand, his head bowed.

"Brehon Law," Ciarán said, "has been practiced in Cwillan since the time Déaglán came to claim this land as his own, as it had been the law in his old homeland. Brian Mór had changed or given new interpretations to the old laws. Déaglean also has made changes.

"Under our old laws, we would place an Eric fine against you. But this is a serious matter. Thus, we must deal with it in a serious manner. As acting brehon my judgment is that you will be taken back to the Fortress of Cwillan with us, no longer a free man. Do you understand?"

Without looking up, the thief shook his head.

"Until your kin comes forward, you will remain with us," Feargus said. "Your kin owes me my horses and four gold pieces. There is also the matter of the sword stolen from Vél. That will be returned with one gold piece."

Feargus signaled for the thief to be taken back to their camp.

CHAPTER
THIRTY-TWO

The rain started soon after the trial, beginning as a soft autumn rain, gradually turning to a hard, cold rain that stung the hands and face and chilled the bones.

Feargus and his men welcomed the rain.

If the temperature dropped during the night, they could have snow by morning.

Rónán helped his father, Seta, and Colm set up a canopy over the cook fire. It would give them a place to get out of the rain while they ate.

"What is this stuff made of?" Rónán asked, running his hand over the skin.

"Goatskin, like our tent roof," Donal said in English.

"They skin goats for their hides?" Rónán asked, surprised.

"They keep goats to the south for milk and meat. The hides are cured and traded for goods in places like Solaria, Moll-Dur, sometimes even as far north as Tir

Lú. We keep them for the cheese we can make from the milk. The meat is tough and has to be cooked for a long time to be able to eat it."

That night, Rónán found the tent he shared with his father cold and damp. He was sure he would be awake all night listening to the rain dripping from the trees and hitting the tent roof.

"Who is Feargus's queen?" Rónán asked his father as he settled himself into his bed.

"Niamh, a young lady from the south, pretty in a way."

"A political marriage?"

"Yes," Donal said.

"Was your marriage a political move?"

"No. I loved your mother. I had the land that Fred Tolan left to me, but I was pretty poor. Your grandfather wanted your mother to marry well. In fact, he had the man picked out for her."

"The senator that grandfather talks about now and then?"

"The very same man. It wouldn't surprise me, if Feargus has more children, that he will marry one off to a lord in Wyneth, or perhaps even into the king's family." Donal sighed. "Time to go to sleep, son."

Rónán was thankful that instead of staying awake all night, he slept well and woke the next morning, but not refreshed. Now he was sure he was coming down with something.

Inside their tent, Ciarán was whispering something to Donal.

When Ciarán left, Rónán sat up. "What is going on?"

Donal pulled back the tent flap. Outside, the gray light gave no clue as to how early or late in the morning it was.

"It is still raining. Stay in bed."

Rónán knew something was up. "Wait for me," he said and hurried to put on his clothing. Rónán noticed his father took his cloak, so this time he put on his cloak over his tunic and pulled up the hood.

Under the goatskin canopy, Beon tended the fire and a pot hanging over it to heat water, or perhaps their breakfast.

Rónán followed his father down to the beach. Below, everyone was assembled. What was going on? Had Feargus decided not to take the thief with him? Did he plan to execute him?

On the beach, the Youths stood in the back row, with a warrior at each end. The thief knelt next to the leader of the Youths, his hands still tied behind his back. In the next row were the remaining warriors, Vél, and Dobailein. Next came Seta and Colm. At the front stood Feargus, Ciarán, and Lonán. Before them, stood a man in a long, dark robe. He had the hood pulled back over his shoulders. The rain slicked his hair down and dripped off his beard. Next to him stood a young boy.

"Is that the executioner?" Rónán asked. Even though the man was guilty, he didn't like the thought of having to witness him being put to the sword.

Donal put a finger to his lips. He moved up to stand next to Seta. Ciarán turned. Seeing Donal and Rónán he moved to the left and signaled them forward. Seta and Colm remained in the second row.

The man before them began to speak, his words coming fast. To Rónán it seemed that there was hardly a break between each word. Though now and then he caught the words "thanks," "rain," and "the Father." Gradually it came to him that the man was either a holy man or a priest.

He hoped he would have a chance to speak to him in private.

Across the lake, thunder boomed among the mountains, forks of lightning raked the peaks, the sound rolled across the dark green water to them. The light rain became a downpour. Rónán looked around, thinking the service would be over soon, but to his surprise, no one looked as though they were going to hurry back to their tents.

"Eíst," the holy man said. Rónán didn't catch what he said next, but later heard, "The Father sends us his love."

When Feargus and his father knelt, Rónán knelt too. Glancing over his shoulder, he found that everyone except the two warriors at the back knelt. Up on the ridge, two warriors stood under a tree. They touched their foreheads, then their chests, turned and disappeared among the trees. Facing forward again, Rónán found that neither Ciarán nor Lonán knelt.

The young boy stepped forward and sang a haunting song about life, the gift from the Father, and about his only Son. When the singing stopped, Rónán was glad he had come. He would never forget this morning, kneeling in the rain with his father and brother.

Feargus said a short prayer. The cadence made it sound more like a personal conversation with God. Then the holy man said the benediction, and they stood.

The service over, they returned to their camp.

⤫

Up on the ridge, hidden among the trees, Kyfer and his men watched the service.

"I told you he was a holy man. No harm to us," Dearg said.

"They are crazy to go before their god in the rain," said Kyfer's second-in-command.

"They are not fools. If you had counted the men as they made their way up the path, you would know that there were two warriors missing," Dearg said

"It is said that he is smart, this king. So why were they missing?" Kyfer said to him.

"They are up in the trees, to warn their lord if anyone approaches."

"Soon I will hear from my nephew, and we will make our move." Kyfer studied the young man who he knew only as Dearg. Next to Dearg stood his friend, a young man who was skilled with a bow. Kyfer said, "I want his horses, and his land. You know your part in this."

"There is no need to wait. You will have it all soon," Dearg said. "And soon I will have my díoltas."

CHAPTER
THIRTY-THREE

It was sometime near midnight, Rónán guessed. Without a watch, he was only sure of the time when the sun was at its zenith. His father stirred in the dark, dressed, and left the tent.

Rónán waited.

An hour or so later, perhaps longer, Donal returned. He entered just as quiet as he had left.

"Did you learn anything, Da?"

"Nothing more than I already knew." Donal's voice sounded surprised.

"Where are they, the thieves?"

"Up on the ridge, in a well-wooded area south of here."

Rónán sat up.

"How long have you known this?"

Donal didn't answer him.

"Are we waiting to see who blinks first?" Rónán asked.

"As to your first question," Donal said, "I knew since the morning we went swimming. I thought I saw someone up on the ridge. So I went down and came up again. As I slicked the water from my face and hair, I got a good look at them. It might come to a fight. I hope not."

"And he knows?" Rónán asked.

"He? You mean Feargus?" Donal didn't wait for his reply. "Yes, I told him as we waded back to shore."

Rónán was cold again, or was it just that the tent was cold? He pulled his blanket up and wrapped it around himself.

"So what do we do now?" Rónán asked, as goose bumps rose on his arms.

"Rón, if I could spare Vél to take you back to the portal, I would do so."

"The hell you will. I'm not going unless you go." Rónán sensed rather than actually saw that his father had moved closer. Something soft was pushed at him. "What's this?"

"You sound cold."

"What will you use?"

"My cloak," Donal said. "It won't be the first time I used it as a blanket. Try to get some sleep."

"Just tell me what the holy man or priest has to do with the thieves?"

"He came to tell us that help isn't coming anytime soon. Both Lord Niall and Lord Rónán, the man you were named after, are away from their fortresses. Probably up at Cwillan, on the same mission that Feargus is on. Lun Dubh, the man we met earlier in the week, will go on to the next holding. But..."

"We are on our own here."

"Yes."

CHAPTER THIRTY-FOUR

Seta, Colm, and the young boy who was the priest's helper walked ahead on the path, leading their horses down toward the Great Plains. Further back, Donal walked his horse alongside the priest.

"You seem troubled, my son."

How could he explain to the holy man about what had happened?

"I have caused a great tragedy, Father."

The priest studied Donal's face, but did not comment.

Donal went on. "I was careless in my duty to care for one living in my holding. I am guilty of arrogance and thinking myself over-wise."

The priest stopped. "Abbot Tuathall should hear any confession you need to make, lord."

"Our good abbot is not with us. This is a matter that weights heavy on my heart."

Again the priest studied Donal. "Come, we will talk." He led the way to some rocks under the tall trees that bordered the path. He tied his horse to a bush. Donal let his horse graze in the grass growing along the path. "Tell me what is troubling you, son."

Donal tried to explain what had happened. At the mention of Jenny's name, the priest's eyebrows shot up, but he did not comment. Donal did not feel that he had given a clear account of what had happened to the daughter of his heart.

Seta and Colm came running back along the path. They stopped when they saw Donal sitting with the priest. Both young men relaxed.

"We will wait for you at the head of the path," Seta said.

"We will join you soon," Donal replied.

When they were alone again, the priest said, "No man, even one with the Power, can know what is in another's heart in all matters. In many ways, your son is like you, both of you putting too much on yourself."

"Feargus is our earthly lord. He has to take much on himself."

The priest studied Donal, but kept silent.

"The tragedy is my fault."

"I see no blame in you, son." He gave Donal a sad, knowing smile. "Kneel, son of Déaglán, let me give you the peace you seek."

Donal knelt before the priest, who placed his hand on his head. "In the name of the Father and Son, let this burden be lifted from you. May peace ease your heart, for I find no fault in you in this matter."

"Thank you, Father," Donal said, touched his forehead, then his chest and stood.

Side by side, with their horses walking behind them, they continued down the path.

Before leaving them to take the trail down to the plains, the priest said, "Take care of your sons, Cullan Donal."

Donal stood with Seta and Colm. They watched the priest and his helper ride on across the plains. In the distance, the Judgment Tree was just visible to the naked eye.

CHAPTER
THIRTY-FIVE

After breakfast, Donal took the last of the apples out of a small bag hanging from a tree branch near their tent. He accompanied Feargus to check on their horses. Seta and Colm, Ciarán and his oldest son were with them.

The apples were a gift from a farmer to the north.

As they rode south along the eastern ridge, they met a young boy running along the road. Seeing Donal, the boy appealed to him for help. "My father is need of a farrier, or skilled horseman. His prized mare is in trouble delivering her first foal."

They found the lathered young mare lying on a bed of dry straw in a small barn.

"I am afraid that the foal is in the wrong position," said the farmer.

Donal took over the farmer's place and held her head, stroking her neck to calm her. Vél, stripped to the waist, washed his right arm and hand with hot water and soap. He knelt and reached inside to reposition the foal. It took several tries before he was able to turn the baby horse.

Once turned, Vél pulled gently on the forelegs. First the legs came clear, then the head, nature took over and the foal was delivered. Donal ran his hand along the mare's neck before he released her so she could stand and see to her foal, a fine reddish-brown colt.

In thanks, the farmer had given Donal the bag of apples.

At the horse pens, Donal threw one of the apples to Feargus for Tinreach.

Feargus threw the apple back to him. Puzzled for a second, he threw one apple to Seta and the other to Colm.

The bothers caught the apples and waited.

Feargus smiled at them and nodded.

The young men placed the apples in the pockets of their tunics, saved for later. Donal did not comment on his son's refusal of the apple.

☙

Upon returning to their campsite, Ciarán came over to talk with Donal.

"Will you walk with me to the upper falls?"

"Is that where Feargus has gone to?"

"He wishes to speak with you in private."

They headed back up the main path until they came to the narrow path that ran at an angle uphill. At the top, Feargus sat on the edge of the boulder, only a pace away from the rushing water. The boulder was dry. The wind had shifted, blowing the spray to the far side.

Ciarán joined his son, Lonán, keeping watch by the old stairs.

Donal sat down next to his son.

Below their feet, the water dropped two hundred paces to a deep oval pool before it rushed downstream to the lower falls.

Feargus talked about his queen, his darling son, Fintán, how he hoped to have a daughter. Donal let him talk. Soon enough he would get to the reason they were here.

Feargus fell silent.

The only sound was the roar of the water as it rushed on its way to Lough Airgead.

"Soon the thieves will make their plan," Feargus said. "When we meet them, will you go with the brothers under a standard of truce and speak with them, on behalf of your people?"

His son made it sound as though he was asking, when in fact, he expected Donal to do as commanded.

"Of course, but tell me first what is going on. Why are you here so late? Soon the year will end."

Feargus looked away, sighed, and nodded.

"You miss nothing, do you? After you left with Moya, we had warm weather, unusually warm. Then it turned hot. The rain stopped, and the spring plantings withered in the fields."

"No rain?"

"No rain. Only those close to water could save their crops. The rain during the service by the lake was the first in over three moons," Feargus said. "Food will be short. Many will go without in the winter. If it is a long cold spell, and snow does not come, we will be in worse shape in the spring.

"I was checking with my lords, when we came across the horse thieves and came up here after them."

"I am sure the king of Wyneth would help, if things are better there than here," Donal said.

"Things there are only slightly better than here."

"You will speak to him?" Donal asked.

"I will, if the need arises. But now we must prepare to deal with the thieves."

CHAPTER THIRTY-SIX

The sun was well past its zenith when one of Feargus's sentries brought word that a woman leading a half horse with a child on it was coming up from the plains.

She walked the half horse down toward them. Ruadrí stopped her at the edge of their camp. Feargus sat under a tree on the beachside, playing ficheall with Ciarán, as if he did not have a care in the world.

Now that Donal understood what was going on, he knew Feargus had big problems and why he had refused the apple. He would not give his horse what he could not give his men. The land was dry. Cwillan was in the middle of the worst drought in many summers.

The rain the other day would help, but it was far too late for the summer crops. Everything rested on next year. As it was many would go hungry this winter.

Ruadrí had the youngest of the Youths search the woman for a weapon that she could conceal beneath her apron or shift. When the search was done, he signaled for her to pass on.

Donal watched as she helped the child to dismount. Leaving the half horse with Ruadrí, together, woman and child moved toward Feargus.

Is he really a child? Donal studied the way the boy walked alongside the woman.

"Check the little man."

He was sure that the child was really a midget, dressed to hide his true age.

Ruadrí frowned, hesitated, unsure of what to do. Seta moved forward to check as Donal had requested. The woman made to protest. Frightened, the boy moved closer to her.

Seta looked to Donal.

He nodded.

Seta knelt down to check the boy. Inside the lining of the child's jerkin, he found a dagger.

Seta held it up for all to see.

The woman gave Donal a sour look, made a sign with her fingers, and spat out several words in his direction in her native language. Seta signaled for her to proceed.

"What did she call you?" Rónán asked, moving closer to his father.

"She made the sign against evil and called me a witch."

"Why?"

"How else would I know that the boy is really a midget, not a child? She forgets that a child walks different than a grown man, no matter the size."

Feargus looked up as the two approached him.

"What brings you here?" he asked in her language.

"I came to plead for the release of my husband."

"I cannot, until my horses are returned with the gold owed me."

"We are poor farmers from the south. We had a horse stolen from us and came to find it."

Feargus looked at the child holding onto her skirt and frowned. The child moved behind the woman.

"Tell your leader I will meet with him tomorrow, at the sun's zenith, or I will return to my fortress and take your husband, if that is who he is, with me. My steward knows how to deal with servants."

At his words, the child moved forward. "We want our man back. Let him return with us now, or harm will come to all of you."

"So, my kin is right. You are a little man. You forget, thief, *you* took my horses."

The little man reached behind him. Before anyone could react, he jumped forward with a knife. Feargus, just as fast, leaned forward and struck him, knocking him to the ground. Before he could scramble to his feet, Ciarán placed his foot on his chest and shook his head.

"Tell your leader he must meet with me on the beach, tomorrow, under a standard of truce. We will discuss what is owed to me and what is not owed to your leader," Feargus said. "Now go."

Ciarán reached down and scooped up the little man, pulled the knife from his hand and carried him back to the half horse and placed him on the saddle.

"Go before my lord changes his mind."

Without a word, or a backward glance, the woman led the half horse back the way they had come.

CHAPTER
THIRTY-SEVEN

The next morning, after their meal, Rónán sat by the fire, talking to Vél.

"You were at Carracán," he said. "What became of Darlisca and Artúr?"

"That is something you will have to ask your father."

"Why? Were you not there?"

"After the old fortress was checked that it was not a trap, the gates were repaired. Your father and his retinue moved in. Darlisca and Artúr and the other lords were brought before your father in the courtyard."

Vél stopped to bank the fire.

"And?"

"We were present when the lesser northern lords were tried. When it was Darlisca's and Artúr's turn, everyone was dismissed. Only your father and the three horsemen know what happened."

Rónán decided to change the subject. "Who are the brothers, Seta and Colm?"

Vél looked up, puzzled by the question. He did not answer right away. "Not all here are as fortunate as your father and myself."

That wasn't an answer.

"Why are they here?" Rónán asked.

"They are young men from the north east. They live on a farm with their mother, but in truth, the farm belongs to her brother. His son will inherit everything. Seta and Colm seek their fortune as one of Feargus's men, or as a Guardian, or in service to one of the other lords. If they stay on the farm, they will be no better than servants."

"My father mentioned that this is their last summer with the Youths."

"Yes, he is right. They want to stay together. None of the lords will take both of them on. So, soon they will return to their uncle's farm."

"They have horses. Surely they could seek their fortune elsewhere?"

"Borrowed horses, I am sure," Vél said. "The coin will be paid when they return to the farm."

Rónán excused himself and went to look for his father to ask about what had happened to Darlisca and Artúr. He found Donal behind Feargus's tent.

Donal was standing in the morning sun, shaving. Seta held an oblong piece of polished metal with a fine sheen on it to use as a mirror. Colm held a bowl of water to rinse his blade in.

"What is going on?"

Donal stopped shaving. "I am going to meet with the thieves so we can resolve this problem. In the spring, the passes will be watched. If they return, it will go hard for them."

"Don't do this, Da," Rónán said, forgetting about Darlisca and Artúr.

"Why not? They aren't going to try anything. If they were expecting reinforcements, they never showed up," Donal said as he continued shaving. He paused. "Even if they double their numbers, they are no match against seasoned fighting men."

Rónán stared at his feet. Watching his father shave with a sharp dagger made him nervous.

"Don't worry, Rón. The brothers will be with me."

"Is that supposed to make me feel better?" Rónán asked. He remembered that he had something just as important to talk to his father about. "We need to talk in private."

Donal finished. He cleaned and dried his dagger and slipped it back into his belt sheath. Next, Colm handed him a pair of scissors to trim his hair and mustache with.

"I have to do this, Rón," Donal said. "I know we need to talk...I talked to the priest. It didn't help me at all. So, yes, I know we need to talk."

Why would his father talk to the priest? None of this was his fault. Even though the priest had given him absolution about Jenny, he still carried the guilt of not telling his father about her.

Next, Colm handed Donal a comb. His father glanced in his direction, before he continued with his hair.

"I didn't know tea could go bad," Donal said.
"What?"

"I borrowed some of the tea you brought with you, son. I think it went bad. It has a strange aftertaste to it. Borrow some from Vél."

"I only have a little left. I'll finish it off. If I need more, I will talk to Vél."

"I need to dress now," Donal said as they walked back to their tent.

CHAPTER
THIRTY-EIGHT

Rónán had to admit his father looked like a prince of Cwillan, a Celtic warrior, with his trimmed mustache and hair. Ciarán had presented Donal with a linen tunic and leggings more fitting his station in life.

Feargus's personal groom and horse holder had brushed Donal's horse. The dark stallion's coat glistened in the afternoon sunlight.

After talking to Feargus for some time, his father nodded and walked over and handed Rónán his broadsword and short sword, only taking his dagger with him.

Donal called for the brothers to mount up.

Rónán had a bad feeling about this. As his father rode out, he found himself praying that he was wrong.

Donal, with Seta to his right and Colm to his left, rode forward to meet the riders from the enemy camp. Colm carried the standard of truce. The two riders coming toward them along the beach also carried a standard of truce.

In his mind, Donal counted the enemy. They were many. Perhaps he had been wrong and they had reinforcements. Not that it would help them, they weren't trained fighting men.

Seeing that they were coming with two mares on leads, Donal turned to call to Feargus. Out of the corner of his eye, he saw movement in the front line of mounted riders. The line opened for the briefest second, and a young man stepped forward holding a bow with an arrow notched. Startled, Donal turned back to see what was going on.

There was a swishing noise, then a loud thunk. Pain sheared through his chest.

Someone, or something, had struck him with a force that knocked the air from his lungs. Pain radiated through his body in a wave that forced him to blink back tears. At the same time, he was thrust backward, almost unseated from his horse. He clutched at the reins and his horse's long, silky mane.

Heart attack.

I'm having a heart attack.

Any second now it would be over, and he would grow cold.

He whispered a prayer to the Father for help for Moya and his unborn child.

Seta turned at the sound. His eyes went wide. "Lord!" he cried. "Cullan Donal has been shot."

What was Seta saying?

Glancing down, Donal was puzzled for a second at the shaft with fletching sticking out of his chest. Then it came to him what had happened: the archer had shot him.

Feargus moved to his side, turned his horse so they were facing each other. Ciarán and Lonán protected his back. There was silence all around them. No one dared speak. The thieves went as white as their standard of truce.

Feargus turned in his saddle and broke the silence. "You come under a standard of truce and then shoot one of my men."

Turning back to Donal, Feargus shook his head and placed his palm on Donal's forehead. Feargus bent closer. He was so close Donal saw little flecks of gold in his son's eyes. For a second they were one, their emotions one, as Donal realized what was happening and couldn't help himself. There were other images that he didn't understand.

Feargus said, "Forgive me."

Donal didn't understand what his son meant. A new pain filled his world. As he slipped into darkness, he heard Feargus giving orders, then the sound of metal on metal as swords were drawn.

CHAPTER THIRTY-NINE

Donal expected the bleakness of the Road of Life and Death, not the stygian darkness that came over him. He woke by degrees, knew he was lying on something hard. At the sound of voices, he opened his eyes and tried to speak. Pain radiated along his jaw and neck, silencing him. His chest ached as if a horse had kicked him.

"It is a miracle," Colm said.

"Is the water hot, Beon?" Rónán said, turning toward the fire.

"Yes, lord."

Donal closed his eyes again, then opened them. Pain made him blink back tears. He was lying on the ground by the campfire. From the slant of the sun, not much time had passed since he was shot.

Nearby, the horse thief sat on the ground, tied hand and foot.

"You're awake," Rónán said as he bent over Donal and begin to cut open his tunic.

"What...?"

"I told you not to go. You took an arrow meant for Feargus."

It took a minute before the pain in Donal's jaw subsided enough for him to say, "Better me than Feargus."

Rónán frowned at him. "I am going to have to cut the thong that holds your pouch."

"Why?

"See, it is a miracle," Colm said again.

"Yes, a miracle," Beon said and touched his forehead, then his chest.

"You're lucky. Your wound should be far worse, yet it isn't," Rónán said. "Though it is going to hurt like hell for a long time. Do you want something to bite down on? I'm going to pull the arrow out."

"Just do it."

Donal closed his eyes. Searing pain spread through his body again. Then, thankfully, it was over - at least the worst of the pain. He opened his eyes. Rónán was holding up the arrow with his pouch caught on the tip.

"Beon, bring me the water."

Rónán pulled off the pouch and was about to throw the arrow into the fire. Colm stopped him. "Feargus wants the arrow."

"Why?"

"He will know the maker by the fletching."

Rónán tested the water before cleaning the wound and applying something sticky.

"Sorry, this is all I have. Funny, back home we almost have a drugstore on every corner. Here, there isn't one anywhere." Rónán smiled down at Donal. "Thankfully, it isn't as bad as I feared."

"I don't understand," Donal said as his son bandaged the wound.

"You can thank Moya and her clan. The arrow caught on the pendant inside your pouch, stopping deeper entry. The impact had to feel horrible. It broke the pendant in two."

Donal said a silent prayer in thanks to the Father.

"What is happening?"

"Feargus sent the youngest of the Youths back with us," Colm said.

"Send them back to the ridge to see what is happening," Donal said. "There is some aspirin under my sleeping mat, Rón."

Rónán turned to Beon and told him what Donal had said. "Will you go and get it?"

"Yes, lord."

One of the Youths returned and knelt down by Donal. "The archer is dead. By whose hand, it is hard to know. The thieves' line broke when Feargus and his men charged. They are trying to make it to the Southern Pass, with Feargus and his men in pursuit."

"Feargus said that as soon as you can ride, to go to the village west of here. The priest there can help us," Colm added.

"Did he say that?" Donal asked.

"Yes, lord," Colm said. "I am sure that is why he sent the youngest Youths with us."

"Just relax, Da," Rónán said.

Donal tried to relax, but he couldn't.

What kept going over and over in his mind was what the Youth had said. Did the thieves' line break on purpose to draw Feargus away, perhaps into a trap?

Once the thieves were well away from the camp, would they send men back to free their man?

"Help me up," Donal said.

"Are you crazy?" Rónán said. "You will start bleeding again."

"Colm, help me up," Donal commanded. "I fear we will have visitors soon."

"You think they drew Feargus off and will come back for their man?"

"Yes, Rón, I think they will. And I am wondering why."

Standing, Donal found that if he didn't make any sudden movements or breathe too deep, he could bear the pain. "Rón, bring me a clean tunic. Colm, hobble our prisoner and bring him to me."

Colm knelt down by the prisoner and untied his feet, then retied them, leaving enough rope between his feet so he could stand and walk after a fashion.

Donal drew his dagger.

"I think you will not kill me," the thief said.

"You think wrong then. Now I wonder why you think this?"

The thief just stared at Donal. *He is trying to think up a story to throw me off, mislead me.*

"Because you have lawgivers and your king would not like you breaking those laws."

"You are wrong again. I have the blood of Déaglán and Brian Mór in my veins. I could kill you, and not one of these men would protest. In fact, if asked, they would swear that you attacked me, and I had to defend myself."

The thief forgot he was hobbled and stepped back too fast and almost fell. Colm pushed him forward toward Donal, causing him to stumble into Donal's arms.

"So I am wondering why you are so important?" Donal pushed the thief back, and put his dagger back in his belt sheath. He stepped forward and placed his left hand on the thief's neck as if to speak to him in private. With his other hand, he placed his thumb on the palm and his other fingers on the back of his hand.

It seems like lately, Donal thought, *I have to force too many people to my will.*

It took only a second. Donal broke the contact and pushed the thief away. He needed to conserve his strength.

The thief lay on the ground where he had landed. "What did you do to me?"

"Nothing," Donal said. "It seems we have had an important man all the time. Bring the horses. Beon, you too, I cannot leave you here."

Rónán handed Donal a spoonful of aspirin and a horn cup of water. "This should help, but I can't give you too much because of your wound."

"Colm, can you find Faolán?" Donal asked.

Colm nodded.

"What is your plan?" Rónán asked.

"Colm will see you and the boys to your namesake's fortress, Faolán. Just tell Lord Rónán or his lady who you are."

"You're going back to help Feargus."

Donal nodded.

The other Youth had joined them. He stood with his companion. Both boys looked at each other, than at Donal. They didn't look happy.

Everyone started talking at once.

The Youths would not follow Colm. Rónán wasn't going without Donal. Colm wanted to help his brother, but would do what he was commanded to do, but...It crossed Donal's mind that the easiest plan was to take everyone to safety. If he did, he wouldn't have time to help Feargus.

It was Beon who settled the matter.

"Lord," Beon said, unnoticed until that moment. He was standing with his horse. "I ask of you leave, to go to help my father."

Looking at Beon, who was scared, but still wanted to go to help his father, Donal made his decision.

"We must stay together and move fast."

Donal turned to his son. "I need you to do whatever I say."

Rónán nodded.

❧

Rónán agreed to do what he was told, but it didn't mean he had to like it, at all. He worried about Donal losing too much blood after being wounded with an arrow. It was crazy enough for his father to be up, much less leading a battle charge.

He checked Donal's bandage again before helping him into a clean tunic.

Donal called for his broadsword and short sword. Rónán watched as his father pulled the strap over his head so the scabbard of his broadsword rested along his back, with the hilt just above his shoulder. He stepped forward to offer to help his father mount his horse. Donal refused and mounted as if nothing was wrong with him. His face was drawn and pale as they set out.

Later, Rónán hoped there would be time to talk to his father. Right now was neither the time, nor place.

The thief rode at the front, between Donal and Colm. His hands were tied before him, and his horse had a noose around its neck. Colm held the other end of the rope. Rónán came next, with Beon at his side. The two Youths brought up the rear.

Rónán was seeing a side to his father he never knew existed, yet in his mind, if not in his heart, he knew had to have always been there. He was seeing the young prince who had defeated the northern invaders by out-thinking and out maneuvering them.

੭ᳲ

Up on the ridge, well hidden by the trees, Dearg was shocked, then angered, that Donal still lived and was leading his small party down to the beach.

Dearg fisted his hand at his side and cursed the House of Déaglán. He turned to the woman and little man.

"All is lost," said the little man.

"Not yet," Dearg said as a new plan begin to take form in his mind. "Will you return to your home now?"

"We will."

"You know there is no proof that Feargus is the true king."

"Words very close to treason, my friend," said the little man.

"Not treason, the truth. He was born during the war with the north. No one attended his birth, not his father, not a holy man, or a lawgiver."

Dearg really did not know, but it made an interesting tale.

"If this is true," the woman said, "the other lords should know."

Dearg was pleased with the results of his simple plan: undermine Cullan and his kin another way. By next Bealtaine, the words would have spread throughout the land.

No, all was not lost.

CHAPTER FORTY

Donal slowed his horse as they approached the first body. It was the archer. His sightless eyes stared up into the blue sky. He shook his head. He didn't have time to worry about the dead, or the waste of a young life.

"You okay?" he asked Rón in English. "Don't look if it bothers you."

"I've seen blood before."

Donal noticed, though, that his son did look away.

They hadn't gone much further, when more than a dozen riders came over the sand dune ahead of them. It was too late to try to hide. The leader pointed in Donal's direction. When the riders split, up most of them heading toward the Southern Pass, the rest headed right at Donal and his small party.

Donal stopped his horse, pulled his dagger out, and turned to Beon to give it to him.

Beon shook his head. "My father gave me this before he went to stand with Feargus," he said and pulled from beneath his jerkin a wicked-looking long knife.

Rónán took the dagger instead.

Donal waited until the riders were close before he drew his short sword. Colm and the Youths did the same.

Further down the beach, as Donal watched the retreating horsemen, they stopped at the point where the beach curved around, following the headland.

"Did you see that?"

"See what, lord?" Colm asked.

Donal didn't have time to discuss what he had seen. The rider coming at them stopped three-dozen paces away. The leader moved his horse forward. Donal placed his sword across the thief's chest. "Stad." To his party he whispered, "Watch the ones in the back."

"I wish to speak with you, Cullan."

"So you know who I am. You are probably also surprised to see me here. The time for talking is over. You violated the standard of truce."

"Not us," the leader said as though he truly felt wronged. "It was a man that came with us from Solaria. How could we know he had a blood feud with you?"

"Solaria? How is Lord Baldor?"

"He was well when we left there half a moon ago," the leader said. He looked over Donal's party. "These are mere boys. It would be a shame for them to die here for nothing."

He was right about the boys. They wouldn't be much help in a fight. Even with Colm by his side, in his condition, the odds were against him.

"It would not be for nothing. You have invaded our land and taken from our lord what is not yours. If we die, it will be as true son's of Déaglán." Donal let that sink in.

"The first to die will be your man," he said, motioning to the captured thief.

The men in the back begin to fan out a little. At Donal's words, they stopped. Their leader turned to them and told them to get back in place.

"Listen to him. He will kill me," said the captured thief.

"I will only tell you this once. Throw down your weapons, and move your horses away from them and dismount. Pull the bridles off, and move toward the water."

What happened next was so quick that Donal didn't have time to react - but the Youth to his right did. The dagger flashed by Donal, a silver blur that stirred the air in its passing. The thief at the end screamed and fell to the ground, his knife still in his hand.

The thieves were forced to sit on the beach, where they were tied hand and foot. The saddles were removed and the horses driven off.

As Colm gathered up the bridles to throw into a pile with the saddles, one seemed to catch his attention. He handed it to Donal. The beautiful inlaid silverwork on the headstall most likely belonged to the leader. He had never liked looting, but the Youth had earned it. He tossed the bridle to the Youth who had been quick with his dagger.

Donal didn't want to leave Beon or Rón behind with these men, so he moved his horse over to the leader and said, "I will expect you to be here when I return. If not, it will go hard for your man here."

More men were coming up behind Feargus. Donal needed to warn his son. He picked up the pace.

At the place where the beach narrowed as it followed the curve along the headland, he slowed his horse.

"Colm, move back behind me."

Donal let his horse walk forward as he scanned the ground. This was where the beach began to climb up toward the pass. If there was a trap, this was the place to set it.

He almost missed the rope and let his horse stumble into the trap. At the last second, he saw where the rope had been cut and later retied. Bits of horsehair and blood clung to the thick cord. He reined his horse to a stop and stood in the stirrups. This sent pain radiating through his chest. It was necessary to see what was beyond the rope.

"Give me the prisoner's rope."

Colm moved forward and handed the rope to Donal.

"There is a rope trap before us. Be careful as you cut it."

Donal half expected the rope, when cut, to snap and harm Colm.

Colm slipped from his horse. With his sword, he cut the thick rope that ran from the sand dune to a few paces into the water. The trap would have been set as soon as the first thieves passed through, and lowered when the second group came through, and set again.

Less than two paces further on was a ditch. Two riders lay at the bottom, along with their horses. The moans from the fallen men and cries from the frightened animals trying to rise made Donal angry. He fought down the rage. He had to keep his head clear.

"Rón, see if you can help these men. Beon, stay with him. When you have cared for the men, see to the horses. You know what to do."

Beon nodded.

Donal feared what he might come upon next. This was a living nightmare, his dream come to haunt him. At a walk, Donal moved his horse down into the ditch. Once he cleared the top, he urged his horse forward, letting the animal take the bit and run.

Sand and small stones gave way to hard ground as the path made the turn around the headland and the incline grew steeper. Donal found the battle on a stretch of land that leveled off for a league before angling up into the Southern Pass through the White Mountains.

Though more experienced, Feargus's men had somehow let themselves be divided, probably when the second party came up behind them.

Ciarán was trying to join up with his king. Lonán lay on the ground a few paces away. Further back, Vél and Dobailein were trying to keep the Youths together. To the left, there was more fighting.

The horse thieves, thinking they would be fighting one man, did not take into consideration Tinreach, who would stand with Feargus to the bitter end if necessary.

Above the sounds of fighting men, the cries of wounded men and horses, came a loud crack as Feargus's shield broke in two. He threw the pieces away, pulled out his dagger to use with his sword and fought on. The thief pressing him moved back. Perhaps aware that his skill level was far less than the kings.

If they killed Tinreach, the thieves would have a better chance. But they wanted the silver-white stallion alive. The horse would be symbolic of their defeat of the king of Cwillan.

Like his ficheall playing, Feargus prided himself on being as good or better than any of his men. He fought with a double-edged sword that he handled as if it was part of him. The thieves only hope was to wear him down to the point he made a mistake.

Without turning, Donal told the Youths to see to Lonán. As he rode closer, one of the thieves tried to grab Tinreach's bridle. The result was as brutal as it was swift. The blow sounded like a melon being struck by a mallet. Blood gushed from the man's head and sprayed the stallion's silvery coat as the man collapsed on the ground beneath his hooves.

"The other rope, Colm."

Colm pulled out another rope with a noose at one end. He pulled the noose over the prisoner's head and threw the other end to Donal.

"Stad!" Donal shouted. "Stad!"

Donal moved his horse closer to his prisoner, grabbed the rope just above the running knot, and pulled it up, forcing the thief to sit up tall. Colm joined him in the shout to stop.

Around him, the fighting slowed and stopped. Men turned their startled faces toward him.

"Lay down your weapons," Donal called to them in a no-nonsense voice.

Feargus didn't relax. He waited to see what would happen next. When no one made a move, Donal pulled the rope higher, and was rewarded with a gasp.

In a hoarse whisper, the thief said, "Please, let me speak." Donal nodded and lowered his hand a little.

"Kyfer, this is folly. Will you fight until we are all carrion for the crows to feast on?"

"Help will come," said an older man stepping closer. Donal drew his sword and waited while father and son stared at each other.

"There is no help. Cullan has seen through your plan, Father."

Anger flashed across the old man's face at his son's words. He sighed, and called to his men to lay down their weapons.

One of the thieves, who Donal learned later, had lost his brother to the bite of Feargus's sword, lunged at the king. Donal reached for his dagger, remembering too late that Rón had it.

With a graceful, smooth stroke, as if in a dance and not a fight for his life, Feargus's sword caught the man and stopped him. Blood sprayed onto Feargus. He put his hand up to protect his eyes. Another man lunged at him. Feargus caught the man with the hilt of his sword to the stomach.

The fight was over, almost as if one man, the thieves lowered their weapons to the ground in defeat.

෩

Ciarán hurried over to speak with Donal.

"It is good to see you up, but..."

"I know I do not look well."

"I will send Vél to you," Ciarán said.

"Have him bring water." Donal wished he had the aspirin pouch with him.

Vél brought a water bag. He looked around for his son. "Is my son safe?"

"Your son is safe with Rón, back at the trap. He stood well. I will speak to Abbot Tuathall on Beon's behalf. He should get an education, even if he plans to stay on your farm."

"I thank you, lord. I know he would be pleased to get further training."

Only after Feargus had seen to all his men did he walk over to where Donal waited on his horse.

"This is a welcome surprise," Feargus said. "My brother is a great healer."

"Your brother is seeing to your men at the trap. We need to go back to collect the other prisoner."

"You look pale. I will help you dismount."

"No," Donal said. The aspirin, or his adrenalin high, was wearing off. Soon he wouldn't even be able to ride. "It is best this is over soon."

"Le do thoil," Feargus said.

Feargus gave orders to his men to have the prisoners dig a trench to bury the dead in. He told Donal later he would have a holy man come up here and lay his men to rest in the name of the Father and Son.

After Ciarán saw to his son and helped him mount his horse, he joined Feargus and Donal.

"There are six dead, two Youths and one of our men, three of the thieves, plus those who were foolish enough to try to take you on, Feargus. Four wounded."

"After they dig the trench, march our prisoners back to their companions. Feargus turned to Donal. "Is that not what you did with Darlisca and Artúr?"

What should he tell his son? The truth? That would ruin the myth that had sprung up about that fateful day so long ago. Perhaps he should have marched, or rather dragged, his enemies through the streets of Cwillan behind his horse. It was what they would have done had they been in his place.

"It was many moons ago," Donal said.

Rónán and Beon waited for them at the trap.

"I gave your men what comfort I could. I am sorry. They were beyond my help," Rónán said. "Also the horses. Beon did what I could not."

"We will bury them here with their horses," Feargus said. "Will you help Vél with the wounded?"

"Yes, of course," Rónán said. "Are you all right, Da?"

"The sooner this is over, the better."

They left guards with the prisoners on the beach and moved on. Later, the thieves would be tried in Cwillan.

At the body of the archer, they stopped. Donal glanced down at the young man as he stared up at the sky, a look of surprise frozen on his face. Donal didn't believe that he had taken an arrow meant for Feargus. He didn't want to dismount either, but he needed to get a closer look at the archer. Sensing what he was about to do, Ciarán dismounted and moved forward to help him.

Pain flashed thought Donal's chest. Once dismounted, he said, "Roll the archer over."

Ciarán knelt and rolled the young man over. He had been stabbed in the back by one of his own men. Donal studied the face. He didn't recognize him. The archer could have come from Cwillan, Wyneth, Tir Lú, or further north.

As Ciarán let the body slump back to the ground, a glimmer of something shiny peeked through the sand.

"What is that beneath him? There in the sand?"

"Where?" Ciarán said as he rolled the body over again.

"There near his shoulder."

Ciarán brushed the sand around. For a second the glimmer disappeared. Then it reappeared again as the sand was brushed away. "There is something here." He stood and handed an ornate brooch to Donal.

It was silver overlaid with gold, not as fancy as the misnamed Tara Brooch, but just as beautiful and probably as old, having been handed down from father to son for many generations. Donal recognized the pattern on the four inlaid filigree panels.

He looked around. Could the owner be among the prisoners? Was he unhappy that Donal still lived? It wasn't possible. He had killed Taydan, the owner of the brooch, many years ago.

"What is it?" Feargus asked.

"An old brooch," Donal said. He hesitated giving it to Feargus. Donal chided himself for being superstitious and handed the brooch to his son.

Feargus examined the brooch before tossing it back to Donal. "Ciarán, help Cullan Donal to mount his horse."

Donal shook his head.

"Then I will walk back with you to our camp," Feargus said and dismounted. "You can rest in my tent, and my kin can see to your needs."

Walk they did.

Each step Donal took sent pain radiating up into his chest. He was beginning to get light-headed. The upward path looked endless. Each step was like ten.

Feargus placed his hand on Donal's arm. His son's support was comforting. It gave Donal a new strength.

He was thankful when they reached the top.

"You have the Power?" Donal asked.

"No. You must be drawing strength from me," Feargus said. "My mother is not from the same line as yours."

Donal fell silent, as memories of Aoife filled his mind.

Without looking back, Donal was sure that Ciarán and Feargus's men who weren't seeing to the wounded or prisoners followed them.

Feargus held the tent flap back for Donal to enter. The young man who saw to the king's needs entered. Feargus dismissed him and helped Donal out of his tunic himself. Only when he had Donal lying on the bed did he call for his brother.

Before Donal slipped into an exhausted sleep, he heard Rón assert himself with Feargus, giving the king orders for what he needed.

Donal closed his eyes.

Chapter Forty-One

On the last day of the year, the Youths gathered dry wood and grass for a bonfire on the beach. To Rónán it seemed as though he had stepped back in time to the days in Ireland when bonfires were lit at Samhain.

Feargus's men dragged several huge old fallen tree trunks down to the beach so everyone would have a place to sit.

Donal was still a little shaky, but was recovering nicely. It was the first day that Rónán had allowed him to get out of bed.

Earlier in the day, Feargus's men had caught a wild boar. The huge animal was placed on a spit over the campfire and slowly roasted. The Youths took turns rotating the boar.

Rónán sat next to his father on the beach as the sky went from blue, to salmon streaked with pink, to purple before it turned to indigo filled with a million stars.

Torches on the ridge were lit. Feargus led the procession down to the beach.

Even in a plain tunic and jerkin, Feargus looked like a king by his stance, the look in his eye, his calm authority. Much as the farmer they helped with the foal knew that Donal was high born, it was not the clothing. Rather, it was how they acted, their body language.

Feargus's men carried the boar down to the beach on long poles. On each side, the Youths walked with torches. Behind the procession walked a lone drummer playing a noisy rhythm to ward off evil spirits.

The boar was placed on another spit closer to the water. All but five torches were put out.

Feargus stood and signaled for silence.

"This is a night to remember our past. For generations we have marked the end of summer at Samhain. But let us not forget that we believe in the Father and Son, that we no longer honor the pagan gods of our forebears.

"Step forward, Ruadrí."

Ruadrí, leader of the Youths, stood as commanded.

Ciarán moved up next to Feargus and handed him a braided leather headband with a blue bead plaited into the center. Ruadrí bowed his head so Feargus could fasten the headband on his brow.

"No longer a garsún, you pass into manhood as one of my trusted men."

Ruadrí stepped back and bowed to the High King. He took the fifth torch from one of his companions and moved around the circle of assembled men. As he came around full circle, he stopped before Rónán.

"What does he want me to do?" he whispered to his father in English.

"You are honored. You cared for the wounded. The men accept you as one of them. Take the torch and light the fire. Thrust it deep so the dry grass underneath catches."

Rónán stood and walked up next to his brother and thrust the torch between the dry timbers.

The fire caught.

Rónán stepped back as the flames raced as if a living creature along the dry timbers. Feargus took him by the arm and moved him further back as the bonfire exploded into life, snapping and crackling, sending sparks into the night air.

Vél and Beon helped carve the boar.

Rónán found the boar meat tender and succulent. He licked his fingers, something he never would have done at home. He was happy, too, when he was handed a second portion. Donal, he noticed, didn't eat as much as he thought his father should. He would have to keep a close eye on him.

Back in the shadows, Lun Dubh stopped to watch the festivities. It would have been easy to slip by the sentries on the ridge. Instead, he made enough noise so they would hear his approach and challenge him.

The sentry was excited to tell him what had happened in his absence. Lun Dubh listened, not telling that he had watched everything from the ridge.

He stood in the darkness, watching Feargus and the one called Cullan Donal. It hurt that he had never attained the status of Guardian. Did Feargus know the truth about him? It did not matter this night. He was content, for now.

Lun Dubh stepped into the light created by the bonfire. At first, startled, everyone fell silent and stared at him.

He bowed to Feargus and his guests.

Feargus stood. "Come, join us in celebration."

Only then did the men make room for him, and the feast went on.

As soon as Lun Dubh had eaten, he walked down the beach with Feargus. Coming back, they stopped to talk just outside the light from the bonfire, closer to the water.

Donal was surprised when Lonán whispered to him that Feargus would like him to join them.

When Donal joined his son, Feargus said to Lun Dubh, "Tell him what you know."

"Lord, I found their camp. From there I followed the trail of three riders, two men and possibly a child. They rode west toward the western mountains. Near the bogland, they split up. I lost the leader a little north of that."

"You have no idea who he is?" Donal asked.

"No, lord, I never gained on him enough to challenge him."

Over protests from Rón, Donal stayed behind to help Vél and Beon with the left over meat and to see to the bonfire. His old friend persuaded him to rest while he worked.

"Who is this man called Lun Dubh?"

Vél looked around. "Beon, it has been long since morning. Go to your bed."

Beon thanked his father and headed back toward their camp.

Vél looked around again. When he was sure they were alone he lowered his voice so only Donal would hear him. "I asked several of the men. They say he trained as an Apprentice a summer gone by. My oldest son might know something. He was at Cwillan that summer. Lun Dubh is good, almost too good, at what he does."

"So why is he a tracker?"

"Not one of the lords would ask for his service."

Including Feargus.

This was a puzzle without an answer. Instead of finding out who Lun Dubh was, Donal found that the tracker was an even bigger mystery.

CHAPTER FORTY-TWO

Rónán woke to the sound of excited voices. His father, who he tried to keep in bed as late as possible, was already up. He dressed and pulled back the tent flap and stepped into a winter morning. Overnight, the temperature had plummeted. Two mornings ago it was Samhain; with the New Year came winter.

He hurried over to Feargus's tent thinking his father was there. Dobailein, running by, stopped long enough to say, "Your father is at the horse pens."

Before going to the pens, Rónán walked out to the beach path. He stopped at the top. He stood amazed; across the lough, the usually gray mountain peaks were frosted with snow or ice. A chill ran down his spine. The storm brewing in those peaks would sweep across the open water, and they would be caught by it, unable to return to the portal. He turned and ran to the horse pens.

He tried to help his father as much as possible getting the packhorses ready. Donal tried to keep up with the younger men, but his wound slowed him down.

They reached the Great Plains before the weak sun began to fade. The wind had picked up, bringing snow with it. Lun Dubh, Ruadrí and half of Feargus's men would escort the prisoners to Faolán bfore returning to Cwillan.

Their smaller party rode another league north before stopping for the night.

In the morning, they rode through the snowstorm until they came to the place where Feargus and his men would go west until they came to the Northern Road. Donal and his party would go along the eastern ridge and cross over to the desert through the White Mountains.

Feargus, Rónán, and Donal dismounted.

Stepping forward, Feargus embraced first his father, then his brother.

"Do not lose yourself in the Great Desert," Feargus said to Rónán. "Take care."

Rónán smiled and nodded at his brother. Feargus was nothing like Robert. Though Feargus would never admit it, he cared for their father very much.

Ciarán dismounted, embraced Donal, and said his farewell to his youngest son, Dobailein.

Before remounting, Donal said, "Take care, Feargus, son of Déaglán. May the Father help you with a plan for the New Year." He stepped closer so they could talk in private. "You will take care of Seta and Colm for me?"

Feargus nodded, and said, "Le do thoil."

CHAPTER FORTY-THREE

The howling wind in the northern White Mountains whipped the snow into deep drifts that made it difficult to ride through. It stung their hands and faces. Already two feet of snow lay on the ground, and still more was coming down. Donal's horse was frightened by the bean sí sound the wind made, forcing him to lead the animal on foot with his head down and a firm grip on the bridle. He hoped to make it easier for his companions to follow in his tracks.

Donal stopped them only long enough to rest the horses and eat a quick cold meal. They had to get over the pass to the eastern side of the mountains before the snow was too deep for the horses.

As the snow grew deeper, everyone, even Rónán, was forced to dismount and lead his horse. Only Beon was allowed to remain on his horse.

Vél took a turn leading the group.

Behind him, Donal heard a strange noise, barely discernible above the howling wind. He turned and looked back. Something was lying on the ground. Hurrying back, he found Beon sitting dazed in the snow.

Beon groaned, "Sorry, I must have fallen asleep."

Donal picked him up, caught the reins of his horse, and carried him forward.

"Do not worry," Donal said, and placed him on the saddle of his horse and handed him the reins.

The endless night went on, until they could barely walk. Their capes and tunics were crusted with snow and ice, their feet frozen in boots, meant for warmer weather.

Sometime well after midnight, the fierce snow and wind grew worse as their path, which had been going upward, now leveled off. They were at the top. Dobailein, at the front, stopped. Donal moved forward and yelled at him to keep going.

They were all thankful when they started the descent on the eastern side, and even more thankful, if it was possible, when the snow slowed to flurries. It was still bitter cold, but the walking was easier.

Donal hoped that they would be able to make up some of the time lost due to the snowstorm. The sun, a light spot in the gray sky, was approaching its zenith as they came out of the pass. It was late afternoon when they entered Vél's holding.

Vél's wife and oldest son welcomed them with warm clothing and hot food, his middle son and a groom took their horses to the stable.

That night, Donal saw that Rónán was comfortable in bed. He brought two mugs of ale, one for Dobailein, the other for his son. Both were laced with an herb that would help them sleep.

By the hearth in the great hall, Donal sat with his friend, over mugs of ale they talked.

Donal reached into the pocket of his tunic, pulled out four silver coins, and handed them to his friend.

Vél looked puzzled.

"For my horse, and in the spring, send two good horses to the brothers, Seta and Colm. Only tell them they are from the man that wishes to sponsor them."

Vél nodded, then returned two of the coins to Donal. "I will see that this is done."

Donal was about to protest.

"Feargus rewards me for the care of your horse."

Donal didn't know what to say to his friend, or about his son. He merely said, "Go raibh maith agat."

Vél nodded, and said, "Watch the garsún in the desert, lord. Strange things happen out there. For this is not a journey he wishes to make."

"Is there something I should know?"

"Last fómhar, my oldest son tracked a stray horse out into the desert. He caught the animal near the watering hole. He planned to spend the night there and return in the morning." Vél stopped and stared into the fire.

"What happened?"

"After midnight, he woke from his sleep to the sound of many voices, and cries of pain or fear. It was hard for him to tell what was going on. He lit his torch, but no one was there, only the voices of those that have gone before."

"Taibhseí?"

Vél nodded.

Could the souls of those who died in the desert still be heard there at night, now ghosts left to wander the endless night?

"I will watch him."

၈ာ

When Donal went to bed, he was surprised that Rónán was still awake. The cup of ale to help him sleep sat untouched on the table by his bed.

"Da, we need to talk."

Donal glanced over at Dobailein, who was sleeping on the other side of the room.

"You need your rest, son. We leave the horses here and walk to the portal," Donal said in English.

Rónán sat up and leaned back against the wall.

"I'm sorry you aren't feeling well. We'll be home soon, but for now, you need to gather your strength."

"I need to ask you something first."

Would Rón blame him for Jenny's death? What his son said next wasn't at all what he expected.

"Do you want me to move out?"

Donal moved over to his son and put his hand on his forehead. He was hot, very hot. He wasn't making any sense either.

"Why would I want you to move out?" Donal asked as he sat down on the bed next to his son.

"Because this is all my fault."

"You caught a bug. There is no blame there."

"Da, Jenny is my fault. I should have told you that she had problems, that she spent time in a clinic a few years back. One of those places that rich people use, everything on the QT."

"No, I think most of it is my fault, son."

"Your fault?" Rónán said and sighed. "She has always been so fragile. Too quiet at times, she was the complete opposite of her half brother, Jason. There was no way you could have known, Da, unless I told you."

Donal listened to his son. Rón must have spoken to the priest as he had. His heart was still heavy with the knowledge that he should have done more for his daughter-in-law.

"We married as soon as we learned that she was pregnant. She seemed better away from her family. She was only close to Joseph. Her father has a mean streak, which explains a lot about Jason."

Rónán tried to reach for his mug of ale, but the table was just out of his reach. He leaned over and caught the edge of the table and dragged it closer. He picked up the mug and took a sip.

"Jenny liked living at Forest Lake. She even liked Alvin. She told me he would make tea for her. He even made tea for me on several occasions, and gave me a bag of tea. He said it was the blend that Jenny liked. I brought it with me."

"Not that strange tea that tastes off?"

"Yes, I finished it just before we left the lake."

Something at the back of Donal's mind stirred, something about the tea. Or was it something about Alvin?

"All I know is her father picked her up that day at the post office and forced her to go home with him."

"What did he do?" Rónán asked.

"I talked to Strickland's chauffeur. He wasn't in the room with Jenny and her father. When the maid brought in tea for them, he had a glimpse of Strickland sitting on the couch with his arm around Jenny. Did she take meds?"

"Not for awhile now. Dear God, the trauma of being forced to go home might have triggered one of her mood swings, causing a relapse that he might have thought should be medicated. He wouldn't do anything to harm her, not on purpose."

Donal was thinking, could they prove anything against Strickland? An autopsy would show what was in her system. But proving how it got there would be another matter. Would it be better to let it go? Or should they force a civil trial for wrongful death?

"Finish your ale and get some rest, son," Donal said. "We will talk about this again when we get home."

CHAPTER FORTY-FOUR

Rónán leaned back against the rock wall.
Donal pulled Rónán's arm over his shoulder. He was very tired, but so was his son and Dobailein. They needed to lie down and rest, but they had to keep going, had to get to the portal before sunrise.

"Can't we rest a bit?"

"Rón, no, we only have a few hours before sunrise."

"Where's Dobailein?" Rónán asked.

"He is waiting for us just ahead. Come on, Rón, time to go."

༄

At Forest Lake, Martin sat down at Donal's desk. He booted up the laptop. At the top ran the ticker symbols for the stock market from a feed from the Robert Long

Agency. Below that, a message said the Dow, Standard and Poor 500, and Nasdaq were down.

The computer beeped, and a warning message came up. It was from Donal. It came up each time Martin turned the laptop on and usually gave him general information. Now a date was flashing in red. It was the date that Donal and his party should have returned by.

Now a new message appeared.

He was to wait for Donal at the portal. There might be a problem, and they would need his help.

Martin would call Mánus and Seán Scanlon before he got ready to go out to the portal this afternoon.

"Are you all right?" Fionn asked.

Martin nodded and ran his hand across his forehead. His fingers came away damp. For the last few days, he seemed too hot and at other times too cold. Of course, he was coming down with something. Fionn sat in the right-hand chair in front of the desk, watching him. Fionn looked as though he had lost this closest friend.

In a way, he had.

It was better to let Donal handle this new problem.

"I'm sorry about the rabbit, Fionn."

"He did it."

Martin knew who *he* was. Alvin.

As he was about to turn the laptop off, a new message came up with the names of several files. The month-end reports that needed checking were still open. On closer inspection, he found they were for cameras at three new locations.

He stared at the screen, before he tried to to move the camera information into a folder. His finger fumbled the keys. It took several tries, but he finally got all the files in a new folder. That done, he slid the laptop aside, moved his teacup, and laid his head down on his folded arms.

All he needed was a little rest. In a minute or two, he would make the call to Mánus and Seán.

CHAPTER
FORTY-FIVE

Donal woke with a start. He hadn't intended to fall asleep. The wind had died down, as it often did at night.

It was pitch-black now.

The dream had seemed so real, as if he was really at the Fortress of Cwillan. He stood in Feargus's private apartment. His son was sitting at a table. His face was thinner, but otherwise, he looked in good health.

Feargus smiled at someone who was outside of Donal's vision. Then his queen, Niamh, came into view. She sat down on his lap. He kissed her, running his hand over her large belly. She was with child again.

Donal shook off the dream and looked around. They had to get going. Time was growing short for them.

Rónán sat against the boulders, wrapped in several blankets, a dark shape against the darker boulders. Donal didn't see Dobailein.

His son needed a doctor. It was slow going now. Rónán could barely walk. The portal wasn't far, but even with Dobailein's help, they might not reach it in time.

Donal told himself not to worry. Martin would be waiting for them at the portal and would help get Rónán up the stairs.

If they didn't make it in time, Donal shuddered to think of what would happen to them. He, much less his son, didn't have the strength to make it back to the watering hole or to Vél's holding.

Donal moved over to Rónán and put his palm on his forehead. Feeling his touch, his son stirred. "Is it time to go?"

"Yes."

"So soon?"

Donal looked around again. "Where is Dobailein?" He didn't wait for an answer. He slipped Rónán's dagger out of his belt sheath and placed it in his hand. "Did he say anything to you?"

"He saw something out there. I think he went to look to see what it was."

It was useless trying to figure out how long Dobailein had been gone. "Keep the dagger handy. I am going to see what is keeping him. Stay here. We'll come back for you."

Donal didn't want to light a torch, but he had to in order to find Ciarán's son. There were several box canyons that he could have wandered down. Donal kept the wall of rock to his right, moving forward with caution. He tried to count his steps as a way to see how far he was going.

He didn't want to leave his son alone too long. There were old myths about the hounds of Hades that hunted here at night. Later the ferocious hounds became the Black and Tan.

At around two hundred steps, he quit counting. He moved through the silent night worried about the waste of time to try to find Dobailein. Donal walked on, checking each side of the canyon. It was hopeless trying to see where the young man had gone.

Should I go back and get Rón and take the chance that we will come across him as we make our way to the portal?

Donal kept on searching.

Dobailein's father, Ciarán, was his closest friend. He couldn't abandon his son out here.

In a small side canyon, he thought he saw something huddled against the boulders. With caution, Donal moved forward, holding the torch up. The wind had risen again, the torch cast strange dancing shadows on the boulders. He was relieved to find it was Dobailein.

Startled, Dobailein swung around, his dagger at hand.

"It is me, Donal."

Dobailein stared at him.

"Did you not see my light?"

Dobailein shook his head. "Sorry, lord...I...saw something in the waning light. I..."

Dobailein was scared out of his wits. What could he have seen out here? Common sense told Donal that nothing lived in this wasteland of sand and heat during the day and cold at night, especially in the winter, when it was cold day and night.

How had Déaglán managed to survive out here with his family and men?

"He is out there waiting to finish what he..." Dobailein's voice trailed off.

"Come, we need to go back and get Rón."

At the mouth of the canyon, a strange noise made Donal stop and turn back the way they had come. For a second he thought he saw something move between the boulders. His blood ran cold. Could it be the spirits of those who never made it across the desert, who left their bones here to bleach in the relentless sun?

Or had someone followed them? Perhaps someone like Lun Dubh, an expert tracker? Donal put the thought out of his mind.

As they turned back to get Rón, Donal was shocked to see torchlight in the distance. When the light went out, he told himself that he had imagined it. Donal kept his torch lit. They could make fast time with it.

ᖇᖇ

"Get up!"

The voice booming out of the night startled Rónán. Had his father come back?

Puzzled, he looked up. There was nothing but darkness, dark sand, and darker boulders.

Something struck his leg.

"I said, get up!"

"Da?"

"Get up! Do not shame your clann this way."

Fear rose in Rónán, this was a voice he had never heard before.

When several torches were lit, he saw that the man was tall, perhaps as tall as his father, only stockier in build. He had piercing eyes and long auburn hair. He wore a shift-like tunic of heavy linen over leggings tied to his legs. His tunic was belted with braided leather with a silver clasp with a running horse design on it.

Beyond the torchlight, there was nothing but darkness. He wasn't even sure where the torchlight came from, though some inner sense told him there were men out there holding torches, watching in the night.

"Eist, amadan. Get up, or I will leave you here in the Fásach Mór, and let the Fear Dubh deal with you."

Rónán struggled to his feet as commanded and slipped his dagger into his belt sheath. The man didn't speak again. He followed Rónán's every movement, as he pulled his blankets around him like a cloak, gathered up his leather carryall and his father's satchel. The man raised his arm and pointed to the east, the direction his father had taken.

As Rónán staggered forward, the man's eyes were on him, watchful that his words were heeded.

He wasn't sure when the torchlight went out. Now he was walking in the dark on a moonless night.

❧

Donal was shocked when he found Rón staggering toward them. His son could barely keep his feet beneath him, yet he kept moving forward.

"I told you, son, to stay put, that I would come and get you."

"I know, but *he* made me do it."

He? Rón was feverish, imagining things.

"How long have you been walking?"

"I don't know." Rónán shrugged his shoulders. "Maybe half an hour, perhaps longer. It is hard to tell, and the man didn't have a watch."

"Man?"

"The man who came and shouted at me to get me up," Rónán said. "So I got up."

Donal placed his hand on his son's forehead. He was even hotter than before. He had imagined the whole thing. "Let me help you. We need to get going."

"His clothes were dirty, but he had a beautiful silver belt clasp with a running horse design on it."

Donal kept walking. He didn't know what to say to his son. He remembered seeing the silver belt clasp once as a young man. It was lost during the war with the north. Not many had heard of it, much less seen it. The clasp was said to belong to Déaglán.

Perhaps he had told Rón about it.

It was a dream, nothing more. The man, the clasp, were all part of a crazy fever induced dream.

Who knew what dreams really meant, why senseless bits of memory came back to haunt you in your dreams.

Soon Donal was almost dragging his son and trying to encourage Dobailein to keep up with them. They took shelter in a natural niche in the rocks. It was snowing again. Donal knew they had to move on, or die here in the Great Desert. After a short rest, he pulled Rónán to his feet and yelled at Dobailein to get up.

"What are you doing?" Rónán asked.

"Didn't you say I reminded you of Red Hugh O'Donnell?"

"Actually, I always saw you as the hero in those old tales," he mumbled.

Donal chose to ignore the remark and said, "Hugh carried his friend in a snowstorm. We aren't far from the portal. Martin will be waiting for us there."

Bending down, Donal lifted his son across his shoulders. He was tired, and his chest had started to throb again. He stopped only once to make sure Dobailein was keeping up with them. He hoped he had the strength he would need to reach the portal. If he had to, he would push his son and foster son through to the other side. But he wouldn't have to. Martin would be there to help him.

The sky was just beginning to lighten to pearl with hints of beige and blue, when they made the turn into the narrow side canyon. Halfway through, they came to the stairs. Donal lowered his son and tried to keep him standing upright.

He was disappointed that Martin wasn't here to meet them.

"I need your help to make it up the stairs."

Rónán didn't speak. He just nodded.

Donal would step up, and then help Rónán up. Dobailein helped steady Rónán while Donal moved to the next step. At this rate, Donal feared it would be close making it to the top in time. Once the sun hit the back wall, the portal closed.

One last step and they were on the huge flat boulder at the top. They had made it in time.

"Thank you, Father," Donal whispered, touching his forehead, then his chest.

Disappointed again.

He had expected Martin to be here at the top. The boulders on the back wall were still invisible; the portal was still open.

Donal pulled Rón forward and pushed him toward the portal. "Martin or Fionn will be waiting for you on the other side."

Rónán disappeared through the portal.

"You next," he said to Dobailein.

Dobailein looked scared.

"Your kin will be on the other side. If it will make you feel better, close your eyes."

Donal pulled Dobailein into position and pushed him through.

Exhausted, Donal fell to his knees, too tired to go on. The pain in his chest threatened to stop him right where he knelt.

He closed his eyes.

The sound was slight.

At first, Donal thought he had imagined it. Opening his eyes, movement to his right caught his attention. He turned his head.

Two children stood near the edge, a girl and a young boy. She had her arm around the boy as if to protect him. The wind swirled around them, lifting their hair, pushing back their cloaks. She opened her mouth and said something to him.

The wind whipped her words away before Donal could make any sense of what she was saying.

She looked familiar, but as tired as he was, he couldn't focus on who she reminded him of.

Donal blinked.

They were gone.

He was alone.

He dragged up his last bit of strength and stood.

Glancing down, he was shocked to see the sun had reached the bottom of the rock wall. Now the boulders were just discernible, and growing darker as the sunlight crept upward.

Soon the portal would close.

Family Tree

<u>Déaglán</u> had four sons and three daughters: Áedán, Keegan, Fintán, Cuilin, Síle, Aine, Caitlín.

<u>Cullan Donal</u> is from the line of Déaglán's oldest son, Áedán, who married one of Brian Mór's daughters.

<u>Donal Tolan</u> (Cullan Donal) with Aoife, had a son, Feargus. By Cynthia Long he had twins, Robert and Donald, and Rónán. He had one child with Moya.

<u>Rónán Tolan</u> had a daughter with Jennifer Strickland named Caitlín Aine.

<u>Cuilin</u> was lost in the Great Desert.

<u>Mánus Seamus Scanlon</u> is from the line of Déaglán's third son, Fintán.

<u>Brid</u> is from the line of Déaglán's third daugher, Caitlín.

GLOSSARY 1 - PEOPLE

Alvin O'Brien - youngest son of Cathal

Aoife - Cullan's second wife

Baldor - lord of Solaria, a desert trading post and oasis

Beon - youngest son of Vél

Brian Mór - Déaglán always referred to Brian Boru as Brian Mór

Callie Weston - works for MSS, an old girlfriend of Donal's

Ciarán - Donal's Guardian – now Feargus's Guardian

Clann - clan

Colm - younger brother of Seta

Cullan Donal	-	Donal Cullan Tolan
Darlisca	-	old enemy from the north,
Dobailein	-	Devlin, youngest son of Ciarán
Donald Tolan	-	Donal's youngest twin
Feargus	-	Ard Ri of Cwillan - Donal's oldest son
Fintán	-	Feargus's son
Fionnbar	-	youngest son of Lord Niall
John Stills	-	Robert Long Agency in Chicago
Liam O'Brien	-	Donal's partner
Lun Dubh	-	tracker
Mánus Scanlon	-	head of MSS - Donal's partner
Martin Rinn	-	Donal's Guardian - son of Lord Rónán
Ruadrí	-	Leader of the Youths
Robert Long	-	Cynthia Long's father
Robert Tolan	-	Donal's oldest twin

Roger Orsnick   -   ex-FBI, Callie's boyfriend

Rónán Tolan   -   Donal's youngest son, AKA Rón

Seta   -   older brother of Colm

Skye Monaghan - accountant – Daughter of Dominic X. Monaghan

Vél   -   horsemen, who lives near the Great Desert

GLOSSARY 2 - PLACES AND WORD MEANINGS

Airgead   - silver

Apprentice - one taking part in an apprenticeship to become a Guardian or join the High King's personal guard

Ard Ri   - High King

Bean sí   - Banshee

Cailíni   - plural of Cailín, young girl

Cuaird   - visit

Díoltas   - revenge

Eíst	-	listen
Estate-linc	-	a super smart-phone developed by MSS to use at Forest Lake, Askeaton. It has an estate link and can be used off estate as a regular phone
Faolán	-	fortress and lake, seat of the Clan of Guardians
Fásach	-	desert
Fásach Mór	-	Great Desert
Fómhar	-	autumn
Garsún	-	boy
Girseach	-	young girl
Le do thoil	-	is often used as "please," but can mean "with your will"
Lough Airgead	-	Silver Lake
Mór	-	great also a name
Púca	-	horse spirit, ghost
Reachtaire	-	steward

Samhain — summers end

Sasanach — Englishman, English language

Selkie — selkies, seals that shed their skin and become human

Stad — Stop

Taibhseí — Ghosts

Tinreach — lightning, the name of Feargus's horse

Tir Lú — Northern part of Cwillan. Land belonging to Artúr and Cullan's aunt. It became part of Cwillan again after the death of Artúr.

Ficheall – This is a game often taken for chess. It is a borad game of sorts the Celtic people brought with them, as well as hurling, to Ireland. Déaglán learned chess from Brian Mór and passed it down to his sons.

When Feargus or Donal are said to be playing ficheall, they are actually playing chess.

Many Thanks

To Heather Murray and Ken Gangwer. Without their
help this book would never have
been possible.
And for Fred P. Wessells, you are missed.

To my father, who gave me the chance and the oppor-
tunity to write this book.

To the real Donal Tolan and Mánus Scanlon,
May the Father and Son keep you safe.
May you never lose your Celtic Soul